# Ayurvedic Healing Methods
# MARMA CHIKITSA

**Ayurveda Health, Happiness & Harmony**

General Editor : Dr. Bal Ram Singh

**Ayurvedic Healing Methods Marma Chikitsa**

Dr. Binod Kumar Joshi & Dr. Geeta Joshi

# Ayurvedic Healing Methods

Dr Binod Kumar Joshi
Dr Geeta Joshi

*Marma Chikitsa*

MLBD
PUBLICATIONS

**MOTILAL BANARSIDASS**
**PUBLICATIONS**
4741/23, Ansari Road, Daryaganj, New Delhi - 110002 (India)
Email: *mlbd@mlbd.com* | *sales@mlbd.com* | *exports@mlbd.com*
Website: *www.mlbd.com*



**Ayurvedic Healing Methods**
**MARMA CHIKITSA**
***by***
**Dr Binod Kumar Joshi • Dr Geeta Joshi**

*First Edition Published in 2021*



Published in India by Motilal Banarsidass Publications

ISBN : 978-81-95055-38-8 (PB)

Printed and bound in India

**Dedicated to**

*Late Dr Ram Lal Sah*

*Our inspiration*

सत्यमेव जयते
वैद्य राजेश कोटेचा
Vaidya Rajesh Kotecha

स्वच्छ भारत
एक कदम स्वच्छता की ओर

सचिव
भारत सरकार
आयुर्वेद, योग व प्राकृतिक चिकित्सा
यूनानी, सिद्ध, सोवा रिग्पा एवं होम्योपैथी (आयुष) मंत्रालय
आयुष भवन, 'बी' ब्लॉक, जी.पी.ओ. कॉम्प्लेक्स,
आई.एन.ए. नई दिल्ली–110023
SECRETARY
GOVERNMENT OF INDIA
MINISTRY OF AYURVEDA, YOGA & NATUROPATHY
UNANI, SIDDHA, SOWA-RIGPA AND HOMOEOPATHY (AYUSH)
AYUSH BHAWAN, B-BLOCK, GPO COMPLEX
INA, NEW DELHI-110023
Tel. : 011-24651950, Fax : 011-24651937
E-mail : secy-ayush@nic.in

## FOREWORD

"Marma Chiktsa" is a comprehensive book written by Dr. Geeta Joshi and Dr. Binod Joshi, which is purely based on their clinical experience for the last three decades.

This book mainly deal with the clinical-based evidences related to certain conditions like headache, *Ama*, knee joint pain, cervical spondylosis, lumbar pain, radiating leg pain, lumbago, and rheumatoid arthritis, etc. The role of *Marma* in preventive and promotive health measures was nicely presented in this book. The information about *Marma* described in Ayurvedic literature is extensively dealt with from modern anatomical perspectives along with the demonstrative illustrations of certain *Marmas*.

The authors have presented the knowledge in a very comprehensive way. I am sure this book will serve as an important reference book. I extend my hearty wishes for this valuable writing venture in the form of this unique book.

**(Rajesh Kotecha)**

New Delhi,
Dated: 06.01.2020

# Preface

For a long time, there had been a need for a book that will deal with the usefulness of marmas for treating diseases. Keeping this in mind we have, in this book, tried to explain with illustrations the different marma points in the body and their methods of stimulation vis-à-vis equivalent to Chinese meridians. The readers can understand that the Chinese knowledge is the cold storage of marma chikitsa and once decoded, different marma points are confirmed.

Description of marmas in Sushrut Samhita around 2500 years ago is a more comprehensive form of what was described in the vedic era. Once an efficient physician stimulates the affected marma by a proper process, patient's self cure mechanism is triggered and the disease is cured. This book provides the simple and specific method of stimulating the marmas as mentioned in Shastras. To understand this one has to go through the shlokas of Chapters of Sushrut Samhita Sharir Sthan.

As per Acharya Sushrut, "Chaturvidhah yastu sirah sharire prayen ta marmasu sannivishtah" i.e, all four siras (Vat, Pitta, Kapha and Rakta) are embodied in Marma. This clearly shows that the methods adopted to stimulate marmas are the same as that of siras and are therefore responsible for treatment.

In our book Vedic Health Care System published in the year 2002 we have unveiled many unanswered questions on 24 Dhamanis, 700 Siras and 107 Marmas of Sushrut Samhita. This is why many researchers and authors from India and abroad honoured us by quoting it. For that we owe them a debt of gratitude. This dignifies and gives us strength.

We have high regards to all the scholars working on marmas and it is a matter of great pleasure and dignity that we all sail on the same boat of marma.

To authenticate our claims, we have quoted shlokas of Sushruta Samhita along with.

As per our long practical medical experience we have tried to provide illustrations for different methods of marma chikitsa. The 107 Dhams of medicine mentioned in Rigveda are the 107 Marmas present in human body. This book is an advancement to authenticate and prove this fact and readers can absolutely be clear that 107 marmas are having special medicinal properties to treat the disease.

# Introduction

For years Vedas have recognized the curing power of Marmas. Rigveda has specified 107 Dhams of medicines to cure the ailments and these medicines originate before the birth of the child. These 107 Dhams are the vital areas available in our body itself instead of earth, and these are the marmas only.

*Ya aushadhih poorva jata devebhyastriyuga purah*
*Manai nu babhrunamaham shatam dhamani sapt ch.*

*Rigveda 10-97-1*

या औषधिः पूर्वाजाता देवेभ्यस्त्रियुगा पुराः,
मनै नु बभ्रुणामहं शतं धामानि सप्त च।

ऋग्वेद 10–97–1

Marmas originate in the body when the foetus is in the mother's womb. This further indicates that the quality of marmas mainly depends on the specific marma quality of parents. In other words, the power of marma depends primarily on parents. Any person can strengthen the marmas by improving aahar-vihar (best quality of food and exercise) and keeping Ras dhatu in excellent condition.

Marma chikitsa was the prime amongst different treatment procedures in the Vedic era. Rigveda clearly indicates this in following verse:

*Ayam me hasto bhagvanayam me bhagvattarah,*
*Ayam me vishvabheshajayo ayam shivabhimarshanah.*

*Rigveda 10-60-12*

अयं मे हस्तो भगवानयं मे भगवत्तरः,
अयं मे विश्वभेषजयो अयं शिवाभिमर्शनः।

ऋग्वेद 10-60-12

"We can cure all the ailments by our efficient hands which are blessed as great lucky power for the welfare of human being".

Marmas are the therapeutic depots of our body. Vital energy (pran) is locked up in marmas in its full power. These therapeutic stimulating areas are the topographical points of our vital organs and body mechanism. By stimulating these selected topographical points, deranged pathophysiology of body can be changed and disease can be cured. Marmas can also be used as a preventive measure, and by regular stimulation of selected marmas, longevity and disease free healthy life can be achieved.

In our previous book 'Vedic health care system', we clearly mentioned that dhamani and siras are not arteries and veins. Instead, they are channels for the circulation of invisible electronically measurable living force 'Ras'. Curing effect of marmas depends on siras, as siras take part to form the basic matrix of marmas.

# Contents

# Marma

Precious use of marmas is described in the Ayurvedic classics and it seems that it has been limited to only one chapter with a very short description. When we study these classics thoroughly in context of marmas, we find in different chapters, the Acharyas give detailed specific treatment for the challenging and incurable ailments. In fact, the whole Sushrut Samhita is the key to the Marma Chikitsa. The deep knowledge of marma chikitsa is hidden in classics like Charak Samhita, Sushrut Samhita and Ashtang Hridaya.

## Marmas are the Topographical Cure Points

Marmas are the topographical cure points of internal vital organs, internal deranged pathophysiology and anatomy. These marmas are thoroughly distributed in our body and have the size of 1 cm to 8 cm (Ardhangul to swapanital kunchit sammit). Classics say that affected marma can be recognized by its painful and tender area. By stimulating marmas, disease can be rooted out or can be checked.

मर्माणि मांससिरास्नायवस्थिसंधिसन्निपाताः तेषु स्वभावत एव विशेषेण प्राणास्तिष्ठन्ति, तस्मान्मर्मस्वभिहतास्तान्स्तान भावानापद्यन्ते।

सुश्रुत शारीर 6/15

*Marmani manssirasnayvasthisandhisannipatah, teshu swabhawat ev visheshen pranastishthanti, tasmanmarmasvabhihatastanstan bhawanapadyante.*

*Sushrut Sharir 6/15*

Marmas are the seats of life. The vital energies (pran) are locked up in these marmas, therefore when they are damaged by the disease, sense organs or related vital organs also get affected. To cure the disease, affected topographical point should be stimulated. For example, if one has radiculopathy of upper arm with neck and shoulder pain and giddiness, it is clear that he is a patient of Ans marma affliction or cervical spondylosis. For this patient stimulation of Ans marma and Ansphalak marma will give relief (exclude TB and cancer). Ans marma lies in the mid point of shoulder in between neck and root of the arm while Ansphalak marma lies on the upper part of the thoracic vertebra (lateral border of 1st thoracic and medial border of scapula on both sides). Stimulation of these marmas can be done by agnikarm (heat treatment or moxibustion), siravedh (stimulation by needles and blood letting in some places), kshar, applying pressure, vaccum therapy (Shringi, Alabu) etc.

The innerconscious 'self' has the wisdom to operate that selfcure mechanism. It comes into operation only when the indicated sira, marma is activated by these methods.

In Abhighat (injury, disease) of Kshipra marma, bleeding will not occur from its points on hand and feet but blood coagulating power decreases or is disturbed and consequently death occurs due to haemorrhage from diseased organ (Sushrut Sharir 6/32). Aaghat of particular marma is not only related to the disease of that area but it affects the total system related to that marma.

According to Acharya Sushrut the finest essence of our consumed food flows through dhamanis and siras and this is called 'Ras'. This Ras is ultramicroscopic live force (param sukshma ras). The presence of this Ras can be judged by perception (anuman) and by the symptoms shown in the body because of fullness or emptiness of channels (dhamanis and siras). The function of ultramicroscopic live force (param sukshma Ras) is to nourish the body. This Ras is responsible for curing the disease, and growth. It is essential for treatment because this Ras has 'Yapan' property.

In our previous book we highlighted the word 'Yapan.' Meaning of Yapan is to extract out or root out the disease. So curing property of Sira, Dhamani and Marma is due to its Yapan property. According to Sushrut, uninterrupted circulation of the living factor Ras (Chinese call it Qi or Chi) is responsible for a disease free life while any obstacle in the circulation of Ras results in disease. The disease is cured if the circulation of Ras is revived. So by our upper said explanation, it is clear that dhamanis and siras are meant for circulation of Ras.

We also highlighted that Sushruta's dhamani and sira are not arteries and veins. Instead, they are the pathways to circulate Ras not visible to naked eye. In Sushrut Samhita Sutra Sthan 14/3 and Sushrut Sharir 9/4-9 where Acharya says about distribution and work of 24 dhamanis, Acharya does not indicate that dhamanis are for circulation of blood only. He instead means that these dhamanis are meant for circulation of Ras, because dhamanis are responsible for smell, speech, respiration, menstruation, defaecation, urination, anaesthesia and hyperaesthesia etc. These facts force us to have firm opinion that Dhamanis are not the vessels of blood circulation but these are the channels or meridians for flow of Ras, which is not detectable in cadaver. The presence of flowing Ras can also be perceived by the symptoms in the body. This continuous flow of Ras is responsible for growth (vardhayati), supports the live forces of the body (dharayati) and cures the disease (yapayati). This is essential for treatment purpose.

According to Acharya Sushrut Dhamanis are 24 in number as shown below:

10 Ascending or Dhatu dhamani

10 Descending or Ashay dhamani

4 Transverse or Tiryag dhamani

# Composition of Marmas

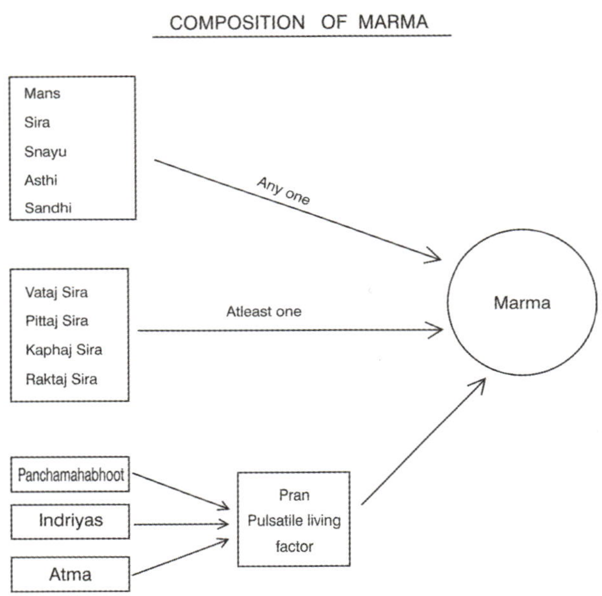


*Marmani mans sira snayvasthisandhisannipatah,*
*teshu swabhavatev visheshen pranastishthanti.*

*Su. Sharir 6/15*

*Chaturvidha yastu sirah sharire prayen to marmasu sannivishtah*
*Snayavasthimansani tathaiv sandheen santarpya*
*deham pratiyapayanti*

*Su. Sharir 6/18*

*Agnih somo vayuh satvam rajastamah panchendriyani*
*bhutatmeti pranah.*

*Su. Sharir 4/3*

# Nabhi Chakra

## Relationship between Nabhi, Dhamani, Sira and Marma

The 'PRAN' of living being resides in nabhi while nabhi depends on prana. Nabhi is surrounded by siras as spikes of a wheel.

नाभिस्था: प्राणिनाम प्राणा: प्राणान्नाभिर्व्युपाश्रिता, सिराभिरावृता
नाभिचश्क्र नाभिरिवारकै:।

सु शारीर 7/5

*Nabhisthah praninam pranah pranannabhirvyupashrita,*
*Sirabhiravrita nabhishchakra nabhirivarkaih.*

*Su. Sharir 7/5*

*Chaturvidha yastu sirah sharire prayen ta marmasu sannivishtah*
*Snayavasthi tathaiv sandheen santarpya deham pratiyapanti*

*Su. Sharir 6/18*

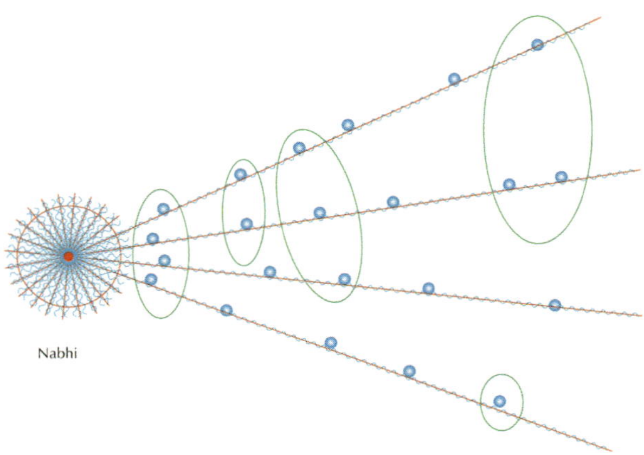


**NOTE :** Dhamani, Sira & Marma are non-anatomical entities.

| Dhamni | (pink line) | Sira | (wavy line) |
|---|---|---|---|
| Marm | (circle) | Having one, two, three or all four types of sira. | |

## Marmas are 107 in number

These therapeutic points are 107 in number. The four types of siras according to doshic distribution are situated in marmas. So stimulation of marmas means stimulation of these siras which are the main constituents of marmas. There are five types of marmas:

1. Mans Marma
2. Sira marma
3. Snayu marma
4. Asthi marma
5. Sandhi marma

The muscle, bone, joints participate to form the structure or matrix of marmas while any of the four types of siras (vata, pitta, kapha and rakta) are seated down together or contained in these marmas. The anatomy and doshic quality of marmas depend on the type of sira.

*Chaturvidha yastu sirah sharire prayen ta marmasu sannivishtah.*
*Snayavasthimansani tathaiv sandheen santarpya deham pratiyapayanti*

*Su. Sharir 6/18*

चतुर्विधा यास्तु सिरा: शरीरे प्रायेण ता मर्मसु सन्निविष्टा:
स्नाय्वस्थिमांसानि तथैव संधीन् संतर्प्य देहं प्रतियापयंति

सु. शारीर 6/18

These 700 siras are specific points on meridians or channels, instead of siras being the veins.

## Topography of Marmas

| | |
|---|---|
| Lower Extremity | 11 × 2 = 22 |
| Upper Extremity | 11 × 2 = 22 |
| Abdomen and Chest | 12 |
| Back | 14 |
| Above clavicle | 37 |

## Distribution of Marmas

| | | | | |
|---|---|---|---|---|
| Lower Extremity | Kshipra | 2 | Janu | 2 |
| | Talhridaya | 2 | Ani | 2 |
| | Kurch | 2 | Urvi | 2 |
| | Kurchshir | 2 | Lohitaksha | 2 |
| | Gulph | 2 | Vitap | 2 |
| | Indravasti | 2 | | |
| Upper Extremity | Kshipra | 2 | Indravasti | 2 |
| | Talhridaya | 2 | Kurpar | 2 |
| | Kurch | 2 | Ani | 2 |
| | Kurchshir | 2 | Urvi (Bahvi) | 2 |
| | Manibandh | 2 | Kakshdhar | 2 |
| | Lohitaksha | 2 | | |
| Abdomen and Chest | Gud | 1 | Stanmool | 2 |
| | Vasti | 1 | Stanrohit | 2 |
| | Nabhi | 1 | Apalap | 2 |
| | Hridaya | 1 | Apastambh | 2 |
| Back | Katiktarun | 2 | Brihati | 2 |
| | Kukundar | 2 | Ansphalak | 2 |
| | Nitamb | 2 | Ans | 2 |
| | Parshvasandhi | 2 | | |

| | | | | |
|---|---|---|---|---|
| Above clavicle | Dhamani marma | 4 | Avart | 2 |
| | Matrika | 8 | Utkshep | 2 |
| | Krikatika | 2 | Shankh | 2 |
| | Vidhur | 2 | Sthapni | 1 |
| | Phana | 2 | Simant | 5 |
| | Apang | 2 | Shringatak | 4 |
| | Adhipati | 1 | | |

## Marmas According to Physical Matrix

As per their physical matrix, these 107 marmas are divided into 5 groups

| | | |
|---|---|---|
| 1. | Mans Marma | 11 |
| 2. | Sira Marma | 41 |
| 3. | Snayu Marma | 27 |
| 4. | Asthi Marma | 8 |
| 5. | Sandhi Marma | 20 |

**MANS MARMA:** All mans marmas are on fleshy portions of the body. These are very important marmas as these are the marmas related to vasovagal shock, cardiac pain and accumulation of blood. According to Acharya Sushrut, when Mans Marmas get afflicted, one loses his senses and his colour becomes dusty.

*Sparsham na janati vipanduvarno yo mansmarmanyabhitaditah syat.*

*Su. Su. 25/40*

स्पर्श न जानाति विपांडुवर्णो यो मांसमर्मन्यभिताडितः स्यात्

सु. सूत्र 25/40

These are :

1. **Talhridaya Marma:** Four in number. One in each limb.

2. **Indravasti Marma:** Four in number. One in each limb.
3. **Stanrohit Marma:** Two in number. One in each side of the chest.
4. **Gud Marma:** One in number. Between perinium and tip of coccyx *(Payu upasth madhye).*

**SIRA MARMA:** These marmas are mainly made of sira which is meant for circulation of *Ras (pran)* as well as transmission of Tridosha and Rakta dosha.

Affliction of sira marma results in bleeding disorders and vitiated vayu causes severe pain, delirium, vertigo, stiff neck and unconciousness.

According to Sushrut sutra 25/36

*Surendragoppratimam prabhutam raktam sraveddvai kshatatashch vayuh*

*Karoti rogan vividhan yathoktanshchinnashu bhinnasvathava sirasu*

सुरेन्द्रगोपप्रतिमं प्रभूतं रक्तं स्त्रवेद्वै क्षततश्च वायुः

करोति रोगान् विविधान् यथोक्तांश्छिन्नासु भिन्नास्वथवा सिरासु

सु. सूत्र 25/36

The total 41 sira marmas are distributed as

1. **Urvi Marma :** Four in number. One in each limb.
2. **Lohitaksha Marma :** Four in number. One in each limb.
3. **Nabhi Marma :** One in number. Situated in abdomen.
4. **Hridaya Marma :** One in number. Situated on thorax. One amongst important trimarmeeya of Charak.
5. **Stanmool Marma** : Two in number. Situated on thorax.
6. **Apalap Marma :** Two in number. Situated on thorax.
7. **Apastambha Marma :** Two in number. Situated on thorax.
8. **Parshvasandhi Marma :** Two in number. On the back, one in each side.

9. **Brihati Marma :** Two in number. On the back, one in each side.
10. **Manya and Neela :** Two Manya and two Neela on the sides of neck.
11. **Siramatrika :** Eight in number making a necklace around the neck.
12. **Phana Marma :** Two in number. One in each side of nostril.
13. **Apang Marma:** Two in number. Lateral to outer canthus of eye.
14. **Shringatak Marma:** Four in number. Located on the head.
15. **Sthapani Marma :** One in number in the centre of the two eyebrows.

**SNAYU MARMA:** Main physical component of snayu marmas is snayu, which is meant for neurological functions. Snayu covers brain cells, sensory and motor neurons, central cortex, nerves, tendons and whole nervous system. According to Sushrut Sutra Sthan 25/37, on affliction of snayu marma, one becomes kyphosed, body parts become unable to do their work, loss of energy, severe pain and delayed recovery from disease.

*Kobjyam shariravayavavsadah kriyasvashaktistumula rujashch*
*Chirad vrano rohati yasya chapi tam snayuviddham manujam vyavasyet*

कौब्ज्यं शरीरावयवावसादः क्रियास्वशक्तिस्तुमुला रजश्च
चिराद् व्रणो रोहति यस्य चापि तं स्नायुविद्धं मनुजं व्यवस्येत्

सु. सूत्र 25/37

The total 27 snayu marmas are described as :

1. **Ani marma :** Four in number. One in each limb.
2. **Kshipra Marma :** Four in number. One in each limb.
3. **Kurch Marma :** Four in number. One in each limb.
4. **Kurchshir Marma :** Four in number. One in each limb.
5. **Vitap Marma :** Two in number. One in each leg.

6. **Kakshadhar Marma :** Two in number. One in each upper limb.
7. **Vasti Marma :** One in number. Situated in abdomen.
8. **Ans Marma :** Two in number. Situated on the back in each side of the shoulder.
9. **Vidhur Marma :** Two in number. Situated in the head below each pinna.
10. **Utkshep Marma :** Two in number. Situated on the head.

**ASTHI MARMA :** All these marmas lie above the bony portion. Main physical component is asthi, so these are called Asthi Marmas. According to Sushrut Sutra 25/39, on affliction of asthi marma there is severe pain in the body and no relief in any position. There is oedema and patient also feels thirsty.

*Ghora rujo yasya nishadineshu sarvasvavasthasu na shantirasti*
*Trishna angsadou shvyathushch ruk ch tamasthividdham manujam vyavasyet.*

*Sushrut Sutra 25/39*

घोरा रुजो यस्य निशादिनेषु सर्वास्ववस्थासु न शान्तिरस्ति
तृष्णाअंगसादौ श्वयथुश्च रुक् च तमस्थिविद्धं मनुजं व्यवस्येत्

सुश्रुत सूत्र 25/39

The total 8 asthi marmas are distributed as:

1. **Katiktarun Marma :** Two in number. Situated on the lower back.
2. **Nitamb Marma :** Two in number. Situated on the back.
3. **Ansphalak Marma :** Two in number, on upper back.
4. **Shankh Marma :** Two in number, on the head.

**SANDHI MARMAS** :These marmas are located over the important joints of the body. Their major physical component is sandhi (union of two or more bones or structures). According to Sushrut Sutra 25/38, on affliction of sandhi marma there is inflammation, severe pain and loss of energy. Joint movements are also restricted.

*Shofativriddhistumula rujashch, balakshayah parvasu bhedshofou*
*Kshateshu sandhishvachalachaleshu, syatsandhikarmopartishch lingam.*

*Sushrut Sutra 25/38*

शोफातिवृद्धिस्तुमुला रुजश्च बलक्षयः पर्वसु भेदशोफौ।
क्षतेषु संधिष्व चलाचलेषु स्यात् संधिकर्मोपरतिश्च लिंगं।

सु. सूत्र 25/38

Sandhi marmas are 20 in number and are distributed over the body as:

1. **Janu Marma :** Two in number, located in each lower limb.
2. **Kurpar Marma :** Two in number, situated in each upper limb.
3. **Kukundar Marma :** Two in number, situated on lower back.
4. **Gulph Marma :** Two in number, one on each lower limb.
5. **Manibandh Marma :** Two in number, one on each upper limb near wrist joint.
6. **Krikatika Marma :** Two in number, situated at the junction of head and neck.
7. **Simant Marma :** Five in number and are situated on the head.
8. **Adhipati Marma :** One in number and is located at the top of the head and is the king of all marmas.
9. **Avarta Marma :** Two in number, situated on the head.

# Classification of Marmas on the basis of their Fatality and Pain Syndrome

According to Acharya Sushrut as four types of siras are contained in marmas and marmas are the seat of life *(Pran)*, when marmas are afflicted, vitiated vayu spreads quickly in these siras and causes severe pain and body loses sense. Likewise vitiated pitta and kapha spreads its pathological doshas as pitta causes high fever, burning and pus formation while vitiated kapha causes heaviness and obstructs channels.

Marmas are classified in 5 groups according to their fatality and pain syndrome:

1. Sadhya Pranhar Marmas (Instant death) - 19
2. Kalantar Pranhar Marmas (death after some time) - 33
3. Vishalyaghna Marmas (Fatal after an injury, needs lifelong treatment for survival till disease exists) - 3
4. Vaikalyakar Marma (One cripples due to deformity of body parts) - 44
5. Rujakar Marma (Typical characteristic excruciating pain) - 8

1. SADHYA PRANHAR MARMAS: These *agneya* marmas are 19 in number. As the agni guna suddenly extinguishes, sudden death occurs due to shock. According to Acharya Sushrut, these marmas require an emergency treatment otherwise the patient may die within seven nights. These are:

| | |
|---|---|
| Shringatak | Gud |
| Adhipati | Hridaya |
| Shankh | Vasti |
| Matrikah | Nabhi |

2. KALANTAR PRANHAR MARMAS: These marmas have *somya* as well as *agneya* property. These are called Kalantar Pranhar Marma as death occurs gradually after some time (15 days to 1 month) due to prolonged illness and lack of proper treatment. Here prognosis is bad mainly due to uncontrolled

haemorrhage, cardiac pain, mental diseases etc. These are:

| | |
|---|---|
| Apalap | Apastambh |
| Stanmool | Stanrohit |
| Simant | Katiktarun |
| Talhridaya | Parshva sandhi |
| Kshipra | Brihati |
| Indravasti | Nitamba |

3. **VISHALYAGHNA MARMAS:** When a pointed weapon is extracted from a wound, it becomes fatal, the spot of wound is called Vishalyaghna. Vishalya means without shalya. These marmas have *vayavya* property. When we think of it deeply it comes out that disease related with vishalyaghna marmas need regular and life long treatment to survive *(yapya)*. In severe attack of disease or injury, it may turn fatal.

   Only two marmas come in this variety, these are:

   Utkshep

   Sthapni

4. **VAIKALYAKAR MARMAS:** These marmas have *somya* property and are called vaikalyakar because there is loss of function and impairment of any part of body or organ as in spondylosis, poliomyelitis, muscular atrophy, hemiplegia etc. These are:

| | |
|---|---|
| Lohitaksha | Neela |
| Janu | Manya |
| Urvi | Phana |
| Kurch | Kukundar |
| Vitap | Kakshadhar |
| Kurpar | Vidhur |
| Ans | Krikatika |
| Ansphalak | Avarta |
| Apang | |

5. **RUJAKAR MARMAS:** These marmas are *Agneya* as well as having vata predominant property. Pain, muscular atrophy and motor impairment are prominent features of Rujakar marmas. These are:

   Gulph

   Manibandh

   Kurchshir

# Marma Chikitsa

Expected results can be achieved by stimulating the marmas. Some marmas get automatically stimulated in physically active persons. Labourers who work under scorching sun or cool conditions also develop immunity against the diseases because their marma points get stronger. On the other hand, a person with sedentary lifestyle is a good harbor for different diseases, their marmas remain weak. By stimulating one or more points for a disease, proper relief can be obtained.

## Simple and selected methods of stimulation of Marmas

According to Acharya Sushrut marmas get afflicted by *aghat*. The meaning of *marmaghat* is diseased or injured marma. There are two types of *aghat*:

1. External or *Bahya Aghat*

   (injury) which can be because of some weapon, sports or physical injury.

2. *Aghaat* or affliction of marma because of vitiation of *doshas* (*dosh vaishamya*).

Such affected marmas can be stimulated by one or more following methods to cure the disease:

1. *Vimlapan* (pressure)/*Peedan*
2. *Vedhan Kriya* (puncturing)

3. *Taap Utpreran*
   (a) *Agnikarm* (by indirect heating)
   (b) *Pottali swed, koshna Tail* (luke warm oil), Steam

4. *Nirvat Prakriya* (Vaccum Suction): According to Sushrut Sharir Sthan 8/26:
   a. By *Pracchan* (Scarification with vaccum)
   b. By *Jalauka* (Leech)
   c. By *Vishaan* (Horn)
   d. By *Alabu* (Gourd)

Sushrut Sutra Sthan 13/4

*Shringi (Vishaan)*: For Vat vitiated diseases

*Jalauka* (Leech): For Pitta vitiated diseases

*Alabu* (Gourd): For Kapha vitiated diseases

## 1. VIMLAPAN/PEEDAN

According to Acharya Sushrut, when disease or *shalya* is not apparent then by *Peedan karma* one can find the tenderness in the related marma. By applying pressure (*vimlapan* or *peedan*) on this marma the disease can be eliminated (See Sushrut Samhita Sutra Sthan 26/12, 27/4 and Chikitsa Sthan 1/22, 1/35-36).

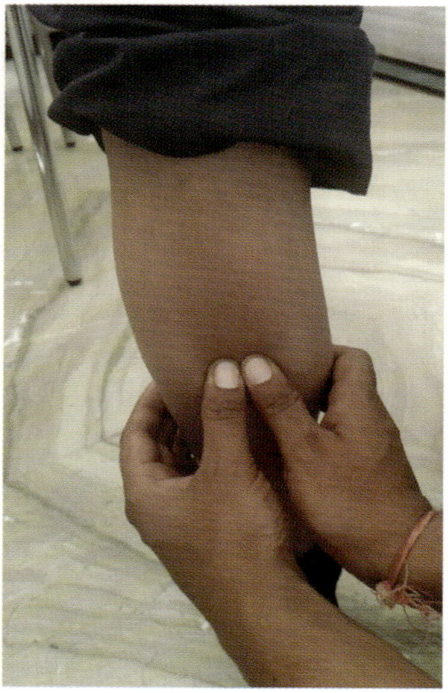

Pressure can be applied by:

1. Thumb (as in Kshipra marma)
2. Index finger (as in Manibandh, Ansa, Stanmool, Apalap, Kakshadhar, Stanrohit, Apastambh, Brihati, Phana, Sthapani, Vidhur, Shankh, Avart, Adhipati etc.)

3. Stimulation by thumbs of both hands is applied on Talhridaya of foot, Urvi and Indravasti because due to hard muscles pressure by one finger is not sufficient to stimulate it. Krikatika marma needs mild single thumb pressure. In muscular areas like Nitamb marma, Kurpar, Ani and Ans marma pressure by 4 fingers give satisfactory results. In *janu sandhigat vaat* pressure of 4 fingers with simultaneous use of thumb gives proper relief because it covers big marma area. Whole palm is used to stimulate Katiktarun marma and in massage of whole spine. Stimulation of Kurch marma also needs all four finger pressure.

## 2. VEDHAN KRIYA

According to Acharya Sushrut, four types of sira (vaat, pitta, kaph and rakta) take part in the formation of marma. *Vedhan kriya* (puncturing) is done for stimulation of marma to eliminate the

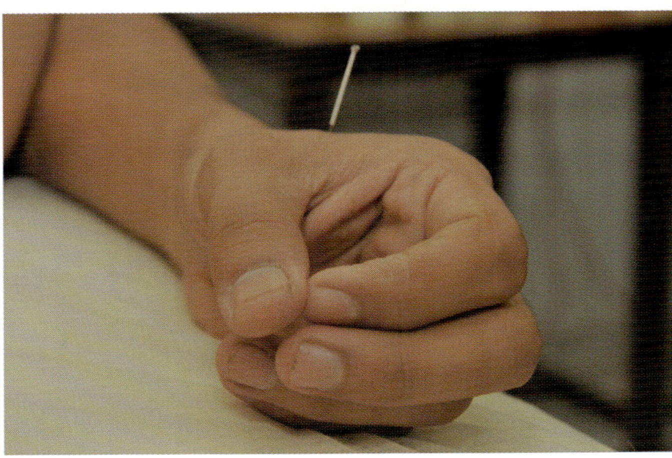

disease. For this a sterile disposable needle is applied to puncture and is left there for fifteen to twenty minutes. Thus interruption caused in flow of *Ras* is restored and later Rakta Dhatu interruption is also cleared, so without blood letting stagnation is cleared. Acharya Sushrut has indicated depth of *vedhan* at different locations (half or one *yava*). The normal acupuncture needles available these days are equally useful. Due to delicate marma sthan instead of blood letting only puncturing also gives desirable results.

## 3. HEAT TREATMENT (*AGNIKARM*)

By heat stimulation of marmas, we can cure the ailment and it is one of the most preferred method. It restores the stagnated flow of *Ras*. In Sushrut sutra 12/4 Acharya suggests different materials

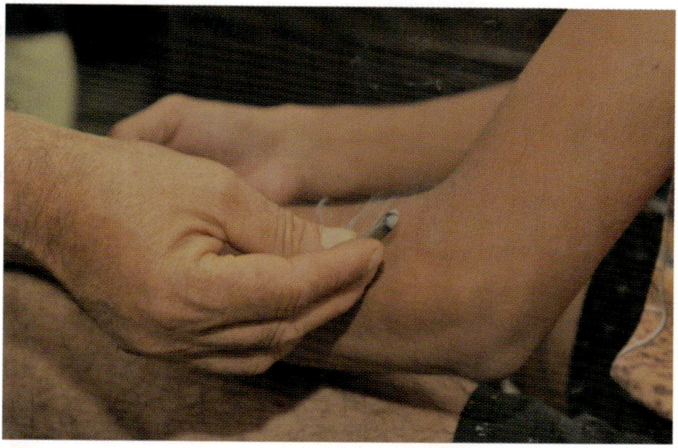

*Agnikarma* (Moxibustion)

used in heat treatment.Goats pellets, *Dhoop* sticks or moxa sticks are the best choice for heat treatment because it does not leave any burn mark. At a distance of half centimeter the affected marma is stimulated by these heated sticks. It is stimulated 5 to 10 times at one point by moving the stick up and down. It can be repeated two or three times in a day depending upon the severity of the ailment. Apart from it the stimulation can be done in circular motion half centimeter above the marma point. Similarly on large joints and broad areas marma points can be stimulated by *pottali swed*, dripping luke warm oil (as in *ekang dhara* or *shiro dhara*), *kati vasti, greeva vasti, janu vasti* and steam sudation.

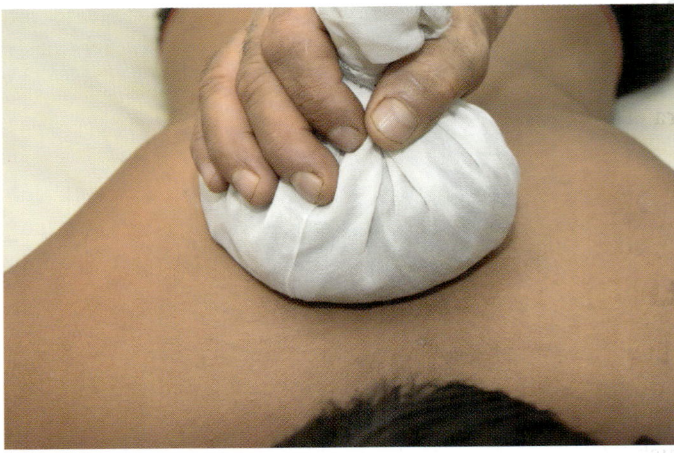

*Pottali Swed*

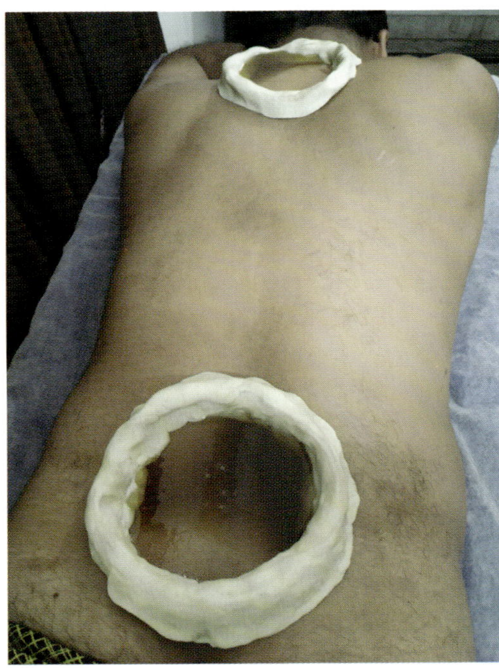

*Kati Vasti and Greeva Vasti*

## 4. NIRVAAT PRAKRIYA

Stagnation can be removed by suction with horn, gourd, Ghati yantra etc. on affected marma.

# Different Marmas and their Stimulation

## TALHRIDAYA MARMA

The literal meaning of Talhridaya is heart present in the lower part of the body or the heart present in palm and sole. The Talhridaya marmas are of mans marma variety and according to Sushrut Samhita Sutra Sthan 25/40 when mans marmas are afflicted, the patient has sensory loss over the involved area and the colour becomes dusty pale (*pandu varn*). According to Sushrut Sharir 6/32 heavy loss of blood from the affected organ causes increase in vata neuro humour resulting in severe pain. There are four Talhridaya marmas two in hands and two in feet. Why did Acharya Sushrut name it Talhridaya? Its answer comes if we think it on meridian theory in which P8 and H8 are in palm and K1 in sole. These are the points to stop pain and bleeding. One of the main causes of pain related to this marma is acute myocardial infarction and angina. So this can be checked by stimulating these two points, specially P8 and H8, and their regular prophylactic use may help to reduce the frequency and severity of angina. It is not a mere coincidence that the Talhridaya marma of Acharya Sushrut corresponds to the meeting point of heart and pericardium meridians (i.e. H8 and P8) of Chinese meridians and the same applies to other marmas as well.

**LOCATION:** Talhridaya marma lies on the centre of the line drawn between the middle finger and centre of palm and sole. These are *sakthi* marmas (marmas of extremities) and are four in number. This marma has half *angul* size (1.0 to 1.5 cm). According to Acharya Sushrut

*Madhyamangulimanupurven madhye padtalasya Talhridayam nam, tatra rujabhirmaranam.*

*Su. Sharir 6/24*

मध्यमांगुलिमनुपूर्वेण मध्ये पादतलस्य तलहृदयं नाम, तत्र रुजाभिर्मरणं

सु. शारीर 6/24

**RESPONSIBLE SIRA BINDU:** Sira of Hridaya and Tal hridaya Dhamani (H8 and P8) in upper extremity and sira of Vrikka Dhamani (K1) in lower extremity.

**INDICATIONS:** Pain and bleeding disorders.

## TALHRIDAYA MARMA CHIKITSA

These three methods of stimulation are beneficial for the ailments mentioned above:

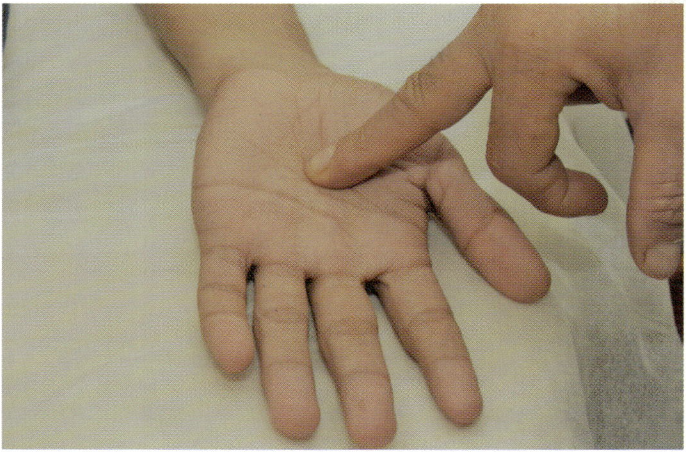

1. **VIMLAPAN (Dabav Bindu Kriya):** Press the point or marma with one thumb in case of palm while the point on sole can be stimulated with the help of both thumbs.

2. **AGNIKARM:** Heating of marma point by burnt *ajasakrit* or moxa/*dhoop* stick 0.5 to 1 cm away from the skin.

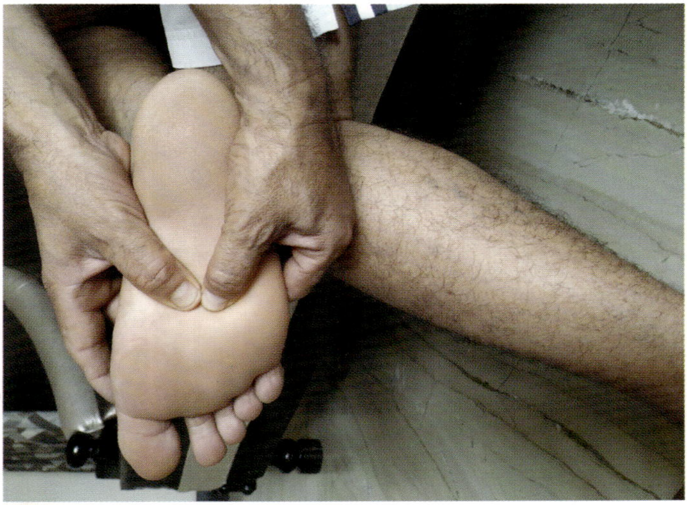

## INDRA VASTI MARMA

It comes under mans marma. It is kalantar pranhar marma i.e. death occurs after some time due to blood loss. Its size is half *angul* (1.0 to 1.5 cm). These are four in number, two in upper extremities and two in lower extremity. Word Indra vasti is used for calf muscle. These marmas are related to blood coagulation system. Quality of this marma is *somya* as well as *agneya*. *Somya guna* coagulates the blood while *agneya guna* prevents stasis. So coagulation depends on the proper balance of these two.

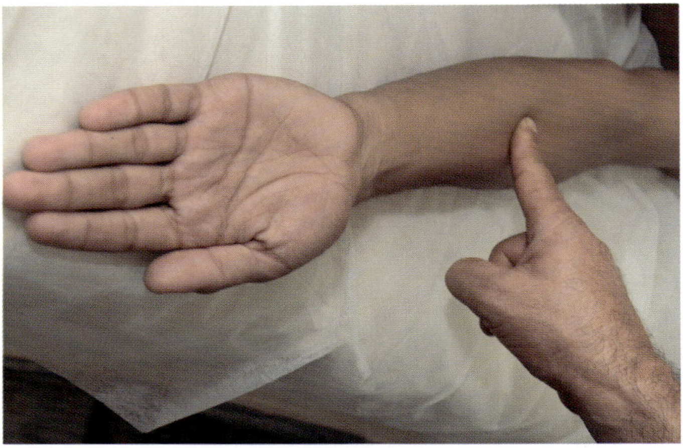

According to Acharya Sushrut

*Parshni prati janghamadhye Indravastih,*
*Tatra shonit kshayen maranam.*

*Su. Sharir 6/24*

पार्ष्णि प्रति जंघामध्ये इन्द्रवस्तिः तत्र शोणितक्षयेण मरणं

सु. शारीर 6/24

Indravasti marma is useful in the treatment of *Apachi*. Acharya Sushrut says for *Apachi*, *siravedh* should be done at two angul below Indravasti Marma. In lower extremity, it is at the centre of calf muscle while in upper extremity, it is in the centre and anterior of the forearm.

**RESPONSIBLE SIRA BINDU:** Sira of Mutrashay and Pittashay Dhamani (UB58 and GB35) in lower extremity and in upper extremity sira of Talhridaya dhamani (P4).

**INDICATIONS:** Blood loss from any part of the body e.g. Haemoptysis, Haemetemesis, haemorrhoids, epistaxis, cardiac pain, palpitation. It must be noted carefully that bleeding will not occur from these therapeutic points. These points are meant to stop bleeding on stimulation.

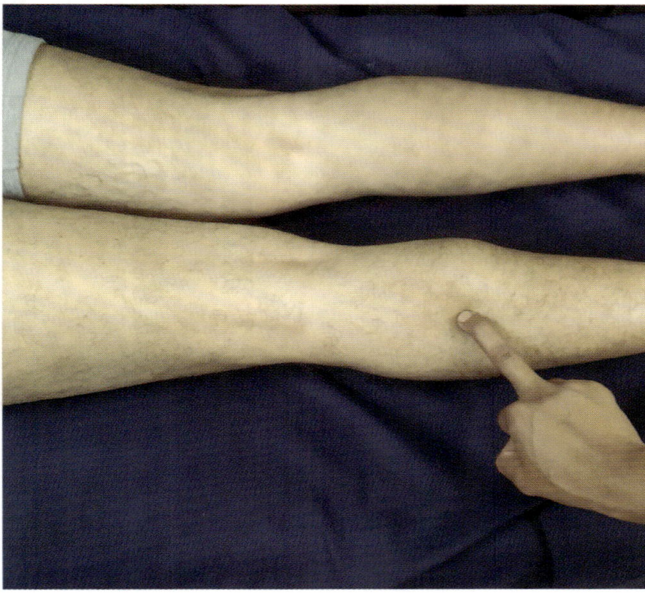

## INDRA VASTI MARMA CHIKITSA

For above said problems, following methods of stimulation are beneficial:

1. VIMLAPAN: Press the above marma bindu with thumb or massage it with til oil.
2. AGNIKARM: Heating of marma point by burnt *ajashakrit* or *dhoop* stick or moxa stick.
3. SIRAVEDHAN: Insertion of needle 0.5 cm deep.

NOTE: As in upper extremity sira of Phuffus dhamani (Lu 6) is adjacent to Indravasti marma area, it has the same indications, likewise in lower extremity sira of Mutrshay dhamani (UB56 and UB57) also have same indications.

# GUD MARMA

Gud marma is mans marma and comes under Sadhya pranhar marma variety because instant death occurs due to vasovagal shock during manipulation of anus in certain procedures. According to Acharya Sushrut

*Tatra vaat-varcho nirasan sthulantra pratibaddham gud naam marm tatra sadhyomaranam.*

*Sushrut Sharir 6/25*

तत्र वातवर्चोनिरसन स्थूलान्त्रप्रतिबद्धं गुद नाम मर्म तत्र सद्योमरणं

सु. शारीर 6/25

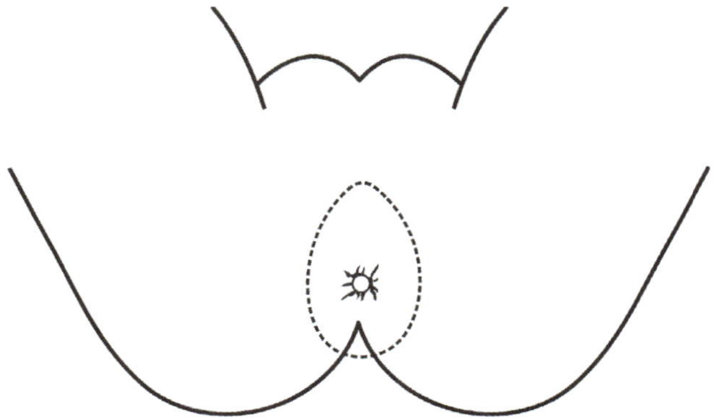

Gud marma is related with large intestine and is responsible for the action of defaecation and expulsion. According to location it is udar marma and is one in number. Its size is *svapanital kunchit sammit* i.e. 6.0 to 7.0 cm in diameter.

LOCATION: The anatomical structure Gud is internal rectal area while gud marma is located midway between perineum and tip of coccyx (payu upasth madhye).

RESPONSIBLE SIRA BINDU: Starting point of Shukra nadi and Artav nadi (Du1 and Ren1)

## INDICATION

*Vatvarchonirasan*

वातवर्चोनिरसन

Hemafecia, Haemorrhoids, Rectal prolapse, pain in the lower back, pain and swelling of anorectal region. As this marma is Agneya, the fire element cools rapidly and vaso vagal shock occurs. The above mentioned pain is due to manipulation during examination of fissure, piles and fistula. The pain subsides immediately on sitz bath due to stimulation of Gud marma points Du1 and Ren1.

## GUD MARMA CHIKITSA

To reduce pain of prolapsed piles, inflamed fissures and fistula, sitz bath of lukewarm water is the best option. Following are the ways of stimulation:

1. AGNIKARM: Heating of these points by *dhoop* stick or moxa stick.

   This can also be stimulated by sitz bath.

## STAN ROHIT MARMA

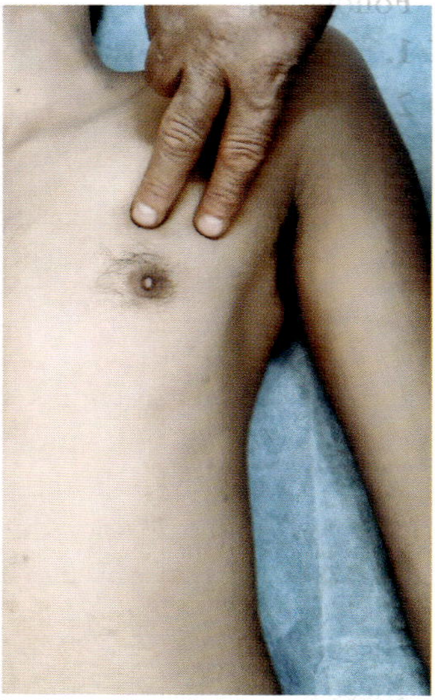

This mans marma lies 2 *angul* above each nipple between 2nd and 3rd intercostal space on anterior part of the chest. On affliction of this marma, cough and breathlessness are the prominent features. Congestion of lungs occurs due to accumulation of blood and it leads to death. According to the location, these are *vaksh* marmas (marmas of chest). Having *somya* and *agneya* quality, this marma is kalantar pranhar (fatal after some time if left untreated). This marma has half *angul* size i.e. 1.0 to 1.5cm.

### LOCATION

*Stanchoochukayorurdhvam dwayangulamubhayatah stanrohitou*

*Su. Sharir 6/25*

स्तनचूचुकयोरुर्ध्वं द्वयंगुलमुभयतः स्तनरोहितौ

सु. शारीर 6/25

**RESPONSIBLE SIRA BINDU:** Sira of Amashay and Pliha dhamani (St16 and Sp20) on both sides.

**INDICATIONS:** According to Sushrut Sharir 6/25

*Tatra lohitpurna koshthataya kasashwasabhyam ch mriyate.*

तत्र लोहितपूर्ण कोष्ठतया कासश्वासाभ्याम च म्रियते

सु. शारीर 6/25

Cough, asthma, pulmonary hypertention and corpulmonale.

## STAN ROHIT MARMA CHIKITSA

Following methods are beneficial for above ailments:

1. **VIMLAPAN:** On its point press with finger or thumb.
2. **AGNIKARM:** Heating of marma by hot water bottle, *dhoop* stick or moxa.

## NEELA - MANYA MARMA

These are sadhya pranhar marmas and are of sira marma variety. These are the marmas of ***urdhvajatru*** (above the clavicle). The size of this marma is ***svapanital kunchit sammit*** (6.0 to 7.0 cm).

**LOCATION:** These are situated on either side of trachea and are related to speech and taste.

*Tatra kanthanadimubhayatashchatasro dhamanyo dve neele dve ch manye*

*Sushrut Sharir 6/27*

तत्र कंठनाड़ीमुभयतश्चतस्रो धमन्यो द्वे नीले द्वे च मन्ये

सु. शारीर 6/27

**INDICATIONS:** According to Sushrut Sharir 6/27

*Vyatyasen tatra mookata swarvaikritam arasgrahita ch.*

व्यत्यासेन तत्र मूकता स्वरवैकृतमरसग्राहिता च

सु. शारीर 6/27

When these marmas are afflicted there is dumbness, changes in vocal cord and tastelessness. When vagus nerve is paralysed, it causes hoarseness of voice and difficulty in swallowing. Hypoglossal nerve is also affected causing hoarseness of voice.

## RESPONSIBLE SIRA BINDU

2 NEELA Sira of amashay dhamani (St 9 on lateral side just on

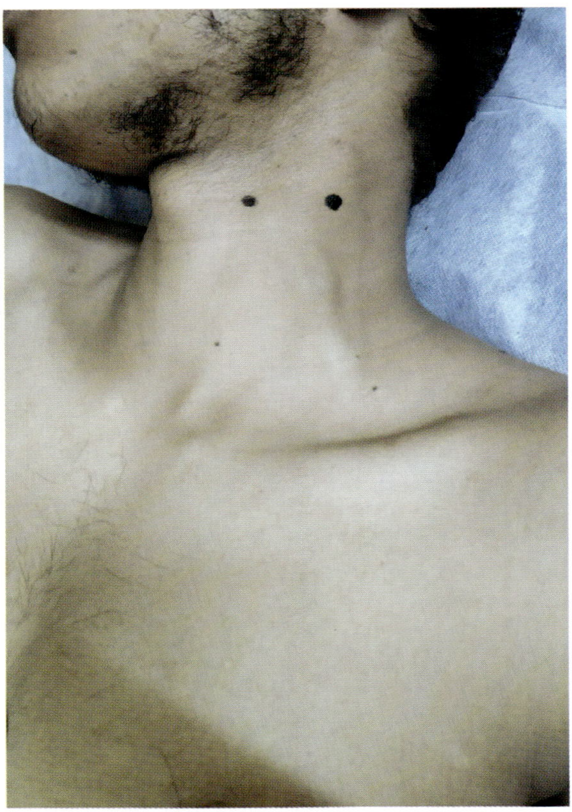

the path of common carotid artery on the level with the tip of Adams apple).

2 MANYA Sira of vrihadantra dhamani (LI 18 on lateral side of neck, level with the tip of Adams apple).

## NEELA MANYA MARMA CHIKITSA

For stimulation of these marmas, following methods are useful:

1. VIMLAPAN: *Vimlapan* or *dabav bindu kriya* is the best method.
2. AGNIKARM: *Agnikarm* by dhoop stick or moxa stick can be done.

## MATRIKA

*Greevayamubhayatashchatasrah sira matrikah tatra sadhyomaranam.*

*Sushrut Sharir 6/27*

ग्रीवायामुभयतश्चतस्त्रः सिरा मातृकाः तत्र सद्योमरणं

सु. शारीर 6/27

On either side of the neck there are 4 sira matrikas. These are Sadhya pranhar marmas and are the marmas of *Urdhvajatru* (above clavicle).The size of this marma is *svapanital kunchit sammit* (6.0 to 7.0 cm). Instant death may be due to carotid sinus syncope.

Matrika means necklace, due to insufficient description a clear cut idea can not be given. These 8 Matrikas may not be related to the points of regular channels but probably they may be points of extra channels.

## SHRINGATAK MARMA

Literally the meaning of shringatak is a place where three or four roads meet. The same is with the definition of Shringatak marma. Shringatak marma is the meeting point of siras which nourish nose, eyes, ears and tongue.

As in Sushrut Sharir 6/27 Acharya Sushrut says:

*Ghranshrotakshijihva santarpaninam siranam madhye*
*Sira sannipatah sringatakani, taani chatvari marmani, tatrapi sadhyomarnam*

घ्राणश्रोत्राक्षिजिह्वासंतर्पणीनां सिराणां मध्ये सिरासन्निपातः श्रृंगाटकानि,
तानि चत्वारि मर्माणि, तत्रापि सद्योमरणम

सु. शारीर 6/27

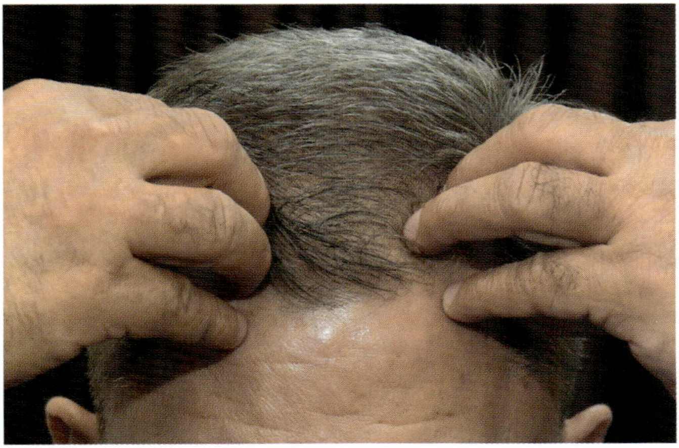

**LOCATION:** These are 4 in number, two on either side of the head. These are ***sadhya pranhar*** sira marma having ***agneya*** property. Its size is 6.0 to 7.0 cm (***svapanital kunchit sammit***).

**INDICATIONS:** Headache, blurring of vision, opthalmalgia, nasal obstruction, epistaxis and tinnitus.

## RESPONSIBLE SIRA BINDU (meridian points)

1st SHRINGATAK: Sira of Mutrashay, Amashay and Pittashay Dhamani (UB4, St8 and GB4)

2nd SHRINGATAK: Sira of Pittashay and Mutrashay dhamani (GB15 and UB5) and Shukranadi (Du22- 23)

## SHRINGATAK MARMA CHIKITSA

For above said ailments, following methods are beneficial:

1. VIMLAPAN: Press with lower end of palm or press with the help of four fingers and thumb collectively. For headache, rhinorrhoea and nasal obstruction, counter irritants like Mentha balm can be rubbed. It stimulates shringatak marma and quickly relieves the symptoms. Due to presence of Shringatak marma on head, wearing of cap is helpful in headache and cold.

For epistaxis, mildly rub its responsible *sira bindu* Shukra nadi (Du 22-23) by *shatdhot ghrit*. (*Shatdhot ghrit* is prepared by a special method in which cow's ghee is washed and rubbed 100 times. Cow's butter can also be used).

2. AGNIKARM: Marma should be stimulated by less heated object which will not make burn marks. Another method is indirect heating by *dhoop*-stick/ moxa.

## APANG MARMA

Literally Apang means outer corner of the eye. Apang marma is related to vision defect, blurring of vision and blindness. These are the marmas of ***urdhvajatru*** (above clavicle) and are two in number.

**LOCATION:** This sira marma is of half angul (1.0 -1.5 cm) size and its location is just below the end of eyebrows.

*Bhrupucchantayoradhoakshnorbahyato apangau.*

*Su.Sharir 6/27*

भ्रूपुच्छांतयोरधोअक्ष्णोर्बाह्यतो अपांगौ

सु. शारीर 6/27

**RESPONSIBLE SIRA BINDU:** Sira of Pittashay and Shleshmashay dhamani (GB1 and Sj23)

**INDICATIONS:** According to Sushrut Sharir 6/27

*Tatrandhyam drishti upghato va*

तत्रान्ध्यम दृष्ट्युपघातो वा

सु. शारीर 6/27

Blurring of vision, blindness, twitching of eye, redness of eye and lacrymation.

### APANG MARMA CHIKITSA

For above said problems, following methods are beneficial:

1. **VIMLAPAN:** Press the Apang marma with index finger or massage in rotatory movement with the help of index finger.
2. **AGNIKARM:** In cosmetic areas like face and scalp etc. marma should be stimulated with the help of less heated object to avoid burn mark. Indirect heating by ***dhoop*** stick or moxa stick is useful.
3. **APPLICATION OF KSHAR:** Apply a small drop of paste

of *kshar* on Apang marma. (*Kshar* prepared by burning dried *Apamarg* plant i.e. *Achyranthus aspera* or *kshar* prepared from lime and Mokha tree i.e. *Schrebera swietenioides*).

4. **APPLICATION OF LEECH:** Application of leech on Apang marma helps to relieve the problems.

**NOTE:** Stimulation by *kshar* and heating its marma area is the method of choice without any hazard.

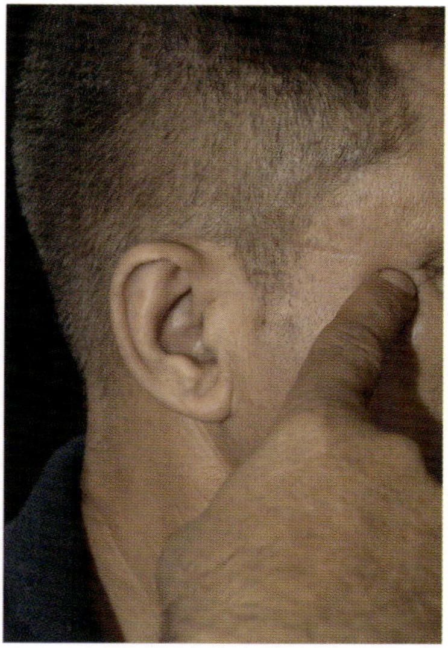

## STHAPANI MARMA

Sthapani marma is the marma of *urdhvajatru* (above clavicle) and is one in number. Literally Sthapani is a space between the eyebrows which is useful to concentrate for meditation. Meaning of *stha* is 'being fixed'. While meditating, the eyes are fixed at this point. This place is also famous due to Lord Shiva's third eye.

**LOCATION:** It lies in between two eyebrows. In Sushrut sharir 6/27 Acharya Sushrut says:

*Bhruvormadhye sthapani, tatrotkshepvat.*

भ्रुवोर्मध्ये स्थपनी, तत्रोत्क्षेपवत्

सु. शारीर 6/27

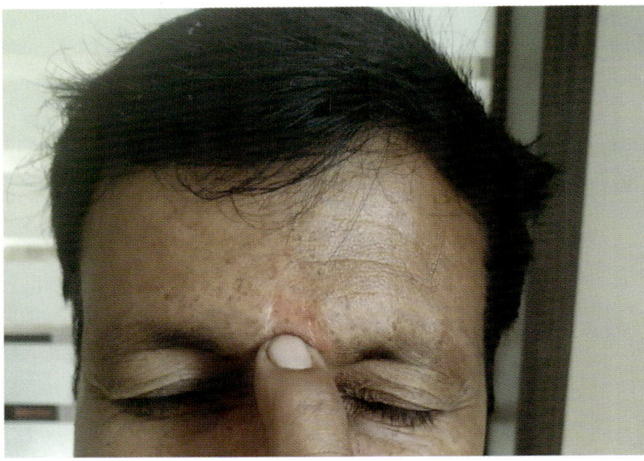

This sira marm is of half ***angul*** size (1.0 to 1.5 cm) and is not in the regular siras (regular 24 dhamanis or meridians) therefore it is extra point. The Chinese call it Yintang.

INDICATIONS: Mental disorders e.g. epilepsy, schizophrenia.

The symptoms of this marma are akin to ***Utkshep***.

## STHAPANI MARMA CHIKITSA

1. VIMLAPAN: Press the Sthapani marma and massage in round movements. For alertness, inner side of both the eyebrows along with sthapani marma area can be stimulated by forceful pinching.

## PHANA MARMA

In our opinion, instead of inner side of nose, Phana Marma should be at the outer side. Since marmas are the topographical cure points, these points of stimulation should be present on skin and should not be located on inner side.

**LOCATION:** These are the marmas of *urdhvajatru* (above clavicle).The size of this marma is half angul i.e.1.0 to 1.5 cm.

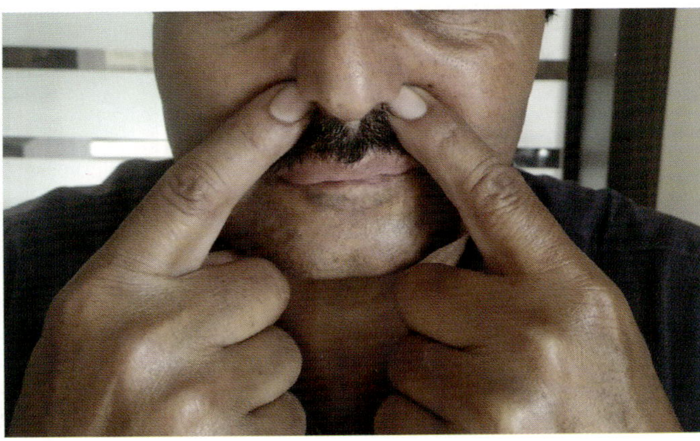

According to *Sushrut Sharir 6/27*

*Ghranmargamubhayatah srotomarg pratibaddhe abhyantartah phane, tatra gandhagyanam.*

घ्राणमार्गमुभयतः स्रोतोमार्गप्रतिबद्धे अभ्यन्तरतः फणे, तत्र गंधाज्ञानं

सु. शारीर 6/27

These marmas are located on either sides of nostrils at the junction of labial skin and nasal membrane. When this marma is afflicted, there is loss of smell.

**RESPONSIBLE SIRA BINDU:** Sira of Vrihadantra dhamani (LI19, 20)

**INDICATIONS:** Anosmia (*Penus*), chronic sinusitis, recurrent rhinorrhoea.

### *PHANA MARMA CHIKITSA*

1. VIMLAPAN: Press the phana marma and massage in round movement. It is also beneficial in treating rhinorrhoea.

## STANMOOL MARMA

According to *Sushrut Sharir 6/25*

*Stanayoradhastad dvyangulamubhayatah stanmoole, tatra kaphpoornakoshthataya(kas shwasabhyam) mriyate.*

स्तनयोरधस्ताद्व्यंगुलमुभयतः स्तनमूले, तत्र कफपूर्णकोष्ठतया (कासश्वासाभ्यां) म्रियते

सु. शारीर 6/25

This sira marma is of one *angul* size (2.0 to 3.0 cm) and is Kalantar pranhar marma.

LOCATION: Stanmool marma resides on each side of chest and is related to chronic respiratory infections. According to Acharya Sushrut, this marma lies at the base of lungs, two fingers below the nipple. Chronic respiratory infections complicate the problem due to filling of cough or sputum.

RESPONSIBLE SIRA BINDU: Sira of Amashay, Pliha and Vrikka Dhamani (St18, Sp17, K 22)

INDICATIONS: *Kaphpoornakoshthataya mriyate.*

कफपूर्णकोष्ठतया म्रियते

Cough, asthma, chronic respiratory infections, pleurisy with effusion.

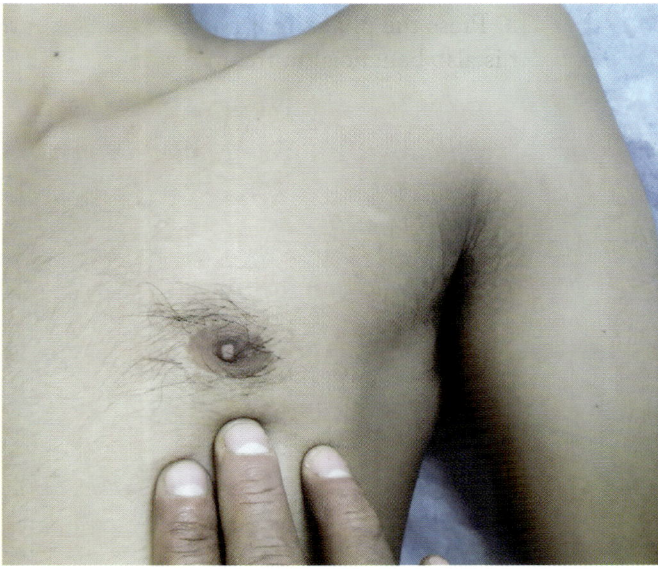

## *STANMOOLA MARMA CHIKITSA*

1. VIMLAPAN: Press the stanmoola marma with thumb or fingers.
2. AGNIKARM: Stimulation of marma by fomentation with hot water bottle, heating pad, moxa/*dhoop* stick.

## APALAP MARMA

Literally the meaning of Apalap is concealing or hiding. Having half *angul* size (1.0 to 1.5 cm) this sira marma is Kalantar pranhar marma (death due to chronic infection).

**LOCATION:** According to Sushrut Sharir 6/25

*Ansakootayoradhastat parshvoparibhagayorapalapou nam tatra rakten pooybhavam gaten maranam.*

अंसकूटयोरधस्तात् पार्श्वोपरिभागयोरपलापौ नाम,
तत्र रक्तेन पूयभावं गतेन मरणं।

सु. शारीर 6/25

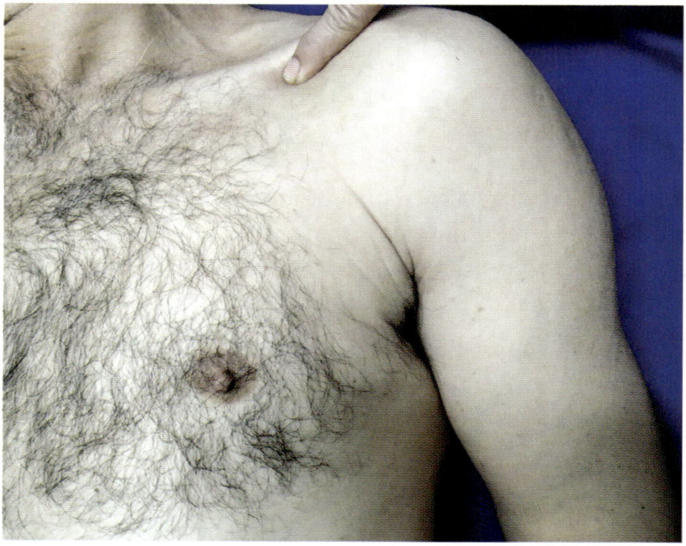

This marma hides itself in the depression made by acromial end of clavicle and upper part of rib cage. These *vaksh marmas* are two in number, one on each side of chest.

**INDICATIONS:** Chronic pulmonary infections.

RESPONSIBLE SIRA BINDU: Sira of Phuffus Dhamani (Lu1)

## APALAP MARMA CHIKITSA

**1.** VIMLAPAN: Press the Apalap marma by finger with rotatory movement.

**2.** AGNIKARMA: Marma can be stimulated by fomentation with the help of small bottle filled with luke warm water. Heating by *dhoop* stick or moxa stick is also useful.

# APASTAMBHA MARMA

This marma is related with cough and asthma. Underneath this marm lies the lateral thoracic artery and vein and the intercostal artery and vein. Position of this marma is in the 3rd intercostal space 8 angul lateral to the midline.

LOCATION: According to Sushrut Sharir 6/25

*Ubhayatroraso nadyou vatvahe apastambhou naam,*
*Tatra vaatpoornakoshthtaya kas shwasabhyam ch maranam*

उभयत्रोरसो नाड्यौ वातवहे अपस्तम्भौ नाम,
तत्र वातपूर्णकोष्ठतया कासश्वासाभ्यां च मरणां।

सु. शारीर 6/25

This marma lies on either side of the chest. According to Acharya Sushrut, vatvah nadis form this marma. Death or critical stage takes place due to invasion of cold damp vayu leading to cough and asthma.

Having half ***angul*** size (1.0 to1.5 cm) this sira marma is kalantar pranhar marma.

RESPONSIBLE SIRA BINDU (meridian points): Sira of Pliha Dhamani (Sp19)"*Nadyou vatvahe*"

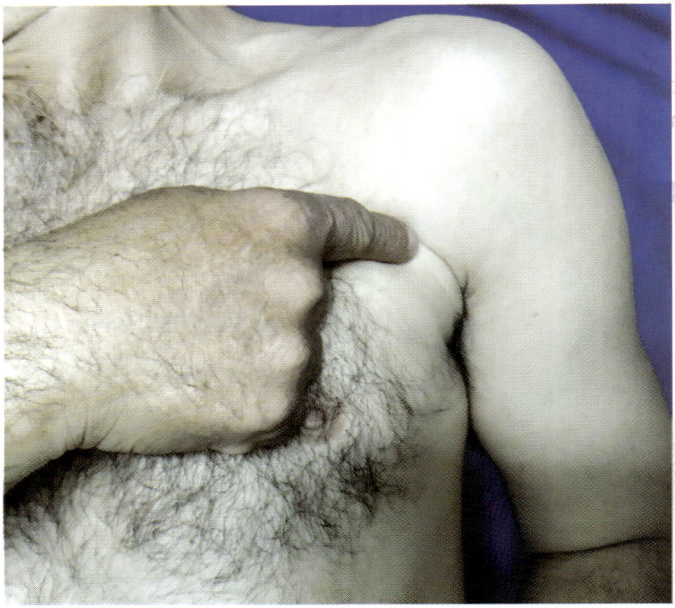

INDICATIONS: Cough, asthma, Pneumothorax caused by chronic infections.

## APASTAMBHA MARMA CHIKITSA

1. VIMLAPAN: Press the marma area by index finger or thumb with rotatory movements.
2. AGNIKARMA: Heat with moxa/***dhoop*** stick.

## HRIDAYA MARMA

Hridaya marma is the seat of three *gunas* namely *Satva, Raja* and *Tama*. This marma is the seat of consciousness and energy and is also related to *manovikar* or psychological disorders. This sira marma is single in number.

**LOCATION:** According to Sushrut Sharir 6/25 Hridaya marma is situated on chest between breasts near the oesophageal end of stomach.

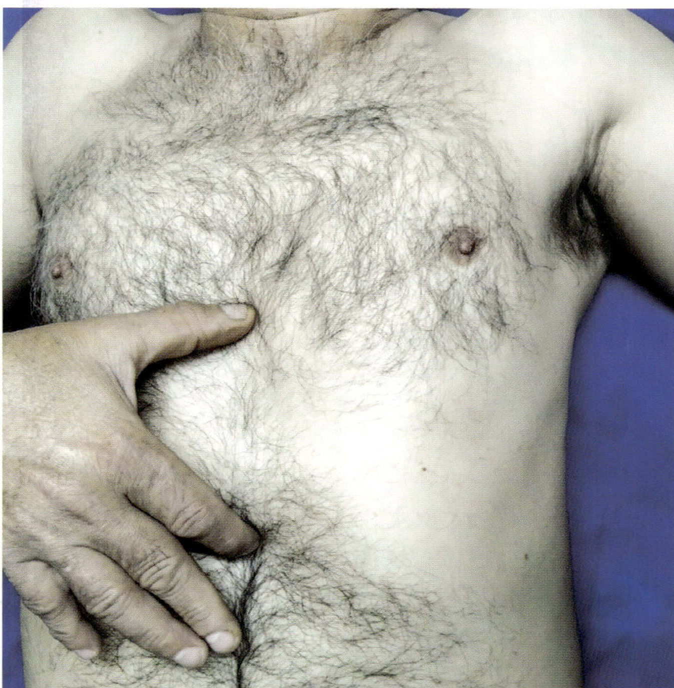

*Stanayormadhyamadhishthayorasyamashayadwaram satvarajastamasadhishthanam hridayam, tatrapi sadhya ev maranam.*

स्तनयोर्मध्यमधिष्ठायोरस्यामाशयद्वारं सत्वरजस्तमसामधिष्ठानं हृदयं,
तत्रापि सद्य एवं मरणं

सु. शारीर 6/25

Having 6 to 7 cm size (*svapanital kunchit sammit*) this *sira marma* is *Sadhya pranhar*.

**RESPONSIBLE SIRA BINDU:** Points of Artav nadi (Ren14, 15 of Chinese acupuncture)

**INDICATION:** Pain in the cardiac region and the chest, mental disorders, palpitations, epilepsy, various cardiac anomalies.

## HRIDAYA MARMA CHIKITSA

1. **VIMLAPAN:** Press the marma by thumb or fingers. Lower end of palm is used for heavy stimulation. Oil massage can be performed.

While describing Hridaya marma, Acharya Sushrut describes its size as *svapanital kunchit sammit* (6 to 7 cm in diameter) and its location is given as *"stanayormadhyamadhishthayo"* which shows that it is not the description of anatomical heart. While thinking on meridian theory, this is the *agramukhi bindu* of heart (Front mu point of Heart). For better therapeutic results, its *Prishthamukhi bindu* (Back Shu point-Mutrashay15-Ub15) should be stimulated simultaneously.

Hridaya marma can be used prophylactically to prevent cardiac anomalies. In CPR Hridaya marma gets stimulated.

## NABHI MARMA

Nabhi is the origin point of live forces. In other words, lines of forces emerge from nabhi. Nabhi is the source point of all 24 Dhamanis and 700 siras. Dhamani and sira of Acharya Sushrut are not artery and veins. Instead, they are channels for the circulation of ultramicroscopic live force *Ras*. It is not blood which flows in Dhamanis while it is *Pran* that circulates in it. During placental circulation, along with blood, foetus also gets its *Ras* or *prana* from mother through nabhi. After child birth, when foetus is detached from placenta, nabhi still remains the origin and source of *pran* throughout the life. According to Sushrut Sharir 6/25

*Pakvamashayormadhye siraprabhava nabhih, tatrapi sadhyomaranam.*

पक्कामाशयोर्मध्ये सिराप्रभवा नाभिः, तत्रापि सद्योमरणं

सु. शारीर 6/25

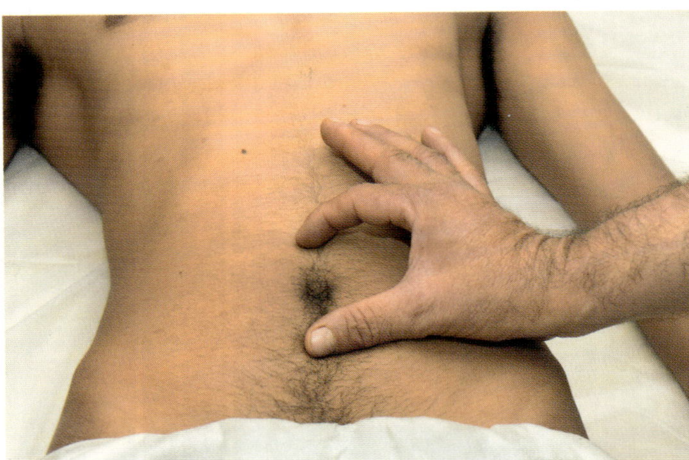

All siras are attached to nabhi from where they spread in all directions. *Pran* resides in nabhi and nabhi depends on *pran*. Nabhi is surrounded by siras as centre of wheel surrounded by spokes. Both dhamanis and siras originate from nabhi. Nabhi is used for centre point or nave of a wheel. During the development of foetus, mother's *Rasvaha naadi* (Channel of ultramicroscopic live force) is attached to nabhi nadi of foetus. This is the time when all these *Urdhva, Adhah and Tiryak dhamanis* get their origin and continue their circulation whole life *(chakra).*

Having the size of 6.0 to 7.0 cm (*svapanital kunchit sammit*) this sadhya pranhar marma is Sira marma.

**RESPONSIBLE SIRA BINDU:** Points of *Artav nadi* (Ren 7, 8, 9 of Chinese)

**INDICATIONS:** Apoplexy, abdominal pain, uterine bleeding.

Due to seat and starting point of circulation of *pran*, it is very sensitive to any external and internal injury causing shock, intense pain and death.

## NABHI MARMA CHIKITSA

1. **AGNIKARMA (Moxibustion):** It is the most selective procedure for its stimulation. Fomentation by hot water bottle gives relief.
2. **Application of Ghati yantra:** Vaccum therapy especially for vitiated vat & kaph.

## PARSHVA SANDHI MARMA

This prishtha marma is kalantar pranhar sira marma having *somya* as well as *agneya* quality. This marma lies on both sides of vertebral column and is having half *angul* size (1.0 to 1.5 cm). According to Sushrut Sharir 6/26

*Adhah Parshvantar pratibaddhou jaghan parshvamadhyayostiryagurdhvam ch jaghanat parshvasandhi.*

अध:पाश्वांतरप्रतिबद्धौ जघनपार्श्वमध्ययोस्तिर्यगूर्ध्वं च जघनात् पार्श्वसंधी

सुश्रुत शारीर 6/26

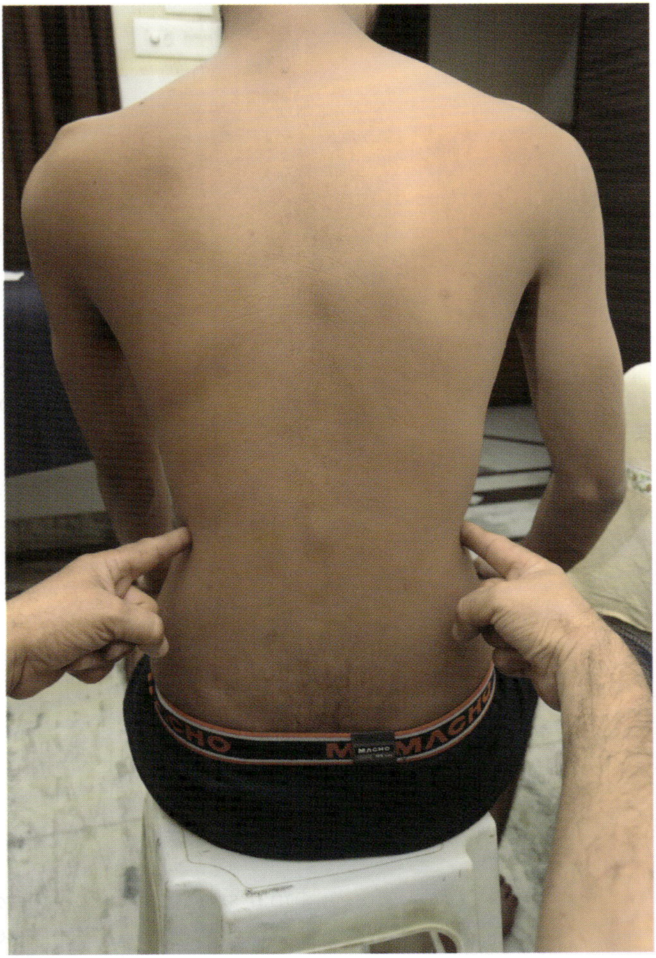

According to above description Parshva sandhi marma has its position below the free end of the 11$^{th}$ rib.

**RESPONSIBLE SIRA BINDU:** Sira of pittashay dhamani (GB 26)

**INDICATIONS:** In Sushrut Samhita sharir sthan 6/26 Acharya Sushrut says:

*Tatra lohitapoorna koshthataya mriyate.*

तत्र लोहितापूर्णकोष्ठतया म्रियते

सुश्रुत शारीर 6/26

This marma has its indication for hepatitis, cystitis, uterine bleeding (menorrhagia, metrorrhagia).

### *PARSHVA SANDHI MARMA CHIKITSA*

For above said indications, following methods can be used:

1. **VIMLAPAN:** Press the marma point with one finger or with the help of all four fingers simultaneously.
2. **AGNIKARM:** Heating by *dhoop* stick or moxa.

## BRIHATI MARMA

This marma has its indication for haemorrhagic disorders of chest. According to Sushrut Sharir 6/26 affliction of this marma causes death due to profuse bleeding from upper respiratory tract (*shonitati pravritti*).

**LOCATION:** This is the marma of back. The two Brihati Marmas lie on each side of vertebral column. If we draw a straight line running backward from the Stanmool marma on either side of vertebral column then Brihati marma can be pointed out. This marma comes under sira marmas. Due to *somya* as well as a*gneya* quality, it is Kalantar pranhar marma and having half ***angul*** (1.0-1.5 cm) size. Its location is 2 inches lateral to the tip of spinous process of the 9th thoracic vertebra.

According to Sushrut Sharir 6/26

*Stanmooladrijoobhayatah prishthavanshasya Brihati, tatra shonitatipravritti nimitterupaddravai mriyate.*

स्तनमूलादृजूभयतः पृष्ठवंशस्य बृहती,
तत्र शोणितातिप्रवृत्तिनिमित्तेरुपद्रवैम्रियते

सु. शारीर 6/26

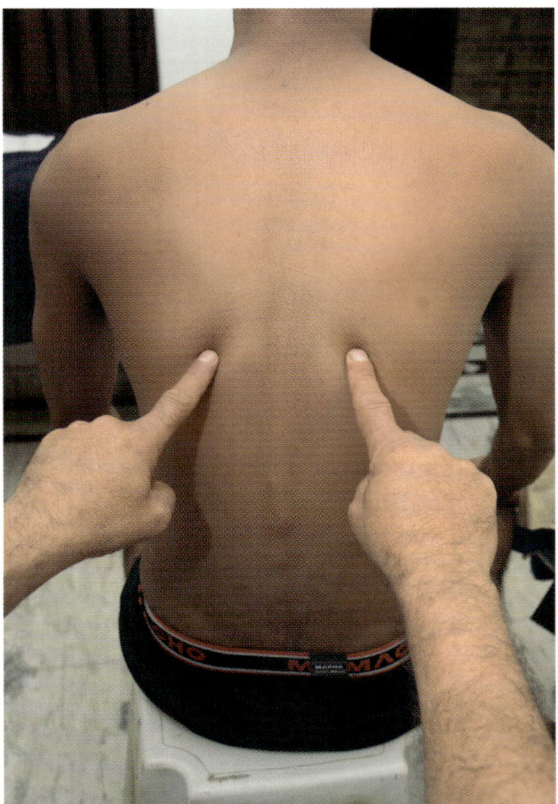

**RESPONSIBLE SIRA BINDU:** Sira of Mutrashay dhamani (UB 18)

**INDICATION:** Brihati marma has its indication for haemoptysis, haematemesis, epistaxis and other respiratory tract haemorrhages.

### *BRIHATI MARMA CHIKITSA*

1. **VIMLAPAN:** Press the Brihati marma by finger with rotating movement. Both the marmas can be pressed simultaneously.
2. **AGNIKARM:** Marma can be stimulated by *pottali swed* after applying lukewarm oil. *Dhoop* stick or moxa stick can be used for heating purpose.

**NOTE:** As sira bindu UB47 is adjacent to Brihati Marma area this also has same indications.

## LOHITAKSHA MARMA

Meaning of *lohit* is blood and *aksha* is axis or the beam of a string which holds the pivot of the beam. So lohitaksha should be the marma of bleeding disorders and it should be in the joint of the arm as well as thigh, and should be responsible for proper movement of arm and leg. This marma lies in extremities (sakthi marm) and is of sira marma variety.

**LOCATION:** According to Sushrut Sharir 6/24, this marma lies above the urvi marma and below the inguinal groove over the inner and uppermost part of the thigh.

*Urvya urdhvamadho vankshansandherurumoole lohitaksh*

उर्व्या ऊर्ध्वमधो वंक्षणसंधेरूरुमूले लोहिताक्ष

सु. शारीर 6/24

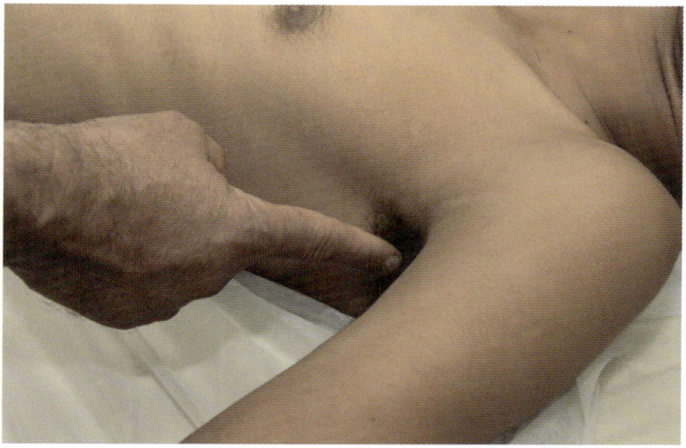

This is vaikalyakar marma causing loss of function of body parts (paralysis). This marm is half *angul* (1.0 to 1.5 cm) in size and is of *somya* as well as *agneya* quality.

## RESPONSIBLE SIRA BINDU (Meridian point):

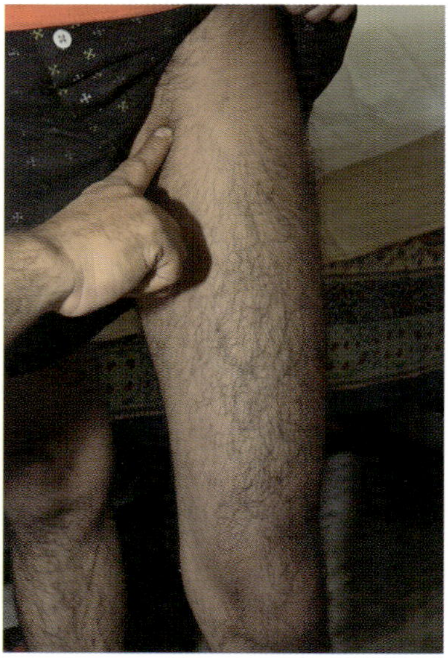

**In upper extremity:** The point which performs the above said function is at the centre of axilla and medial to axillary artery i.e. Sira of Hridaya Dhamani (H1).

**In lower extremity:** Sira of Yakrit dhamani (Liv11)

In lower extremity femoral artery and vein is underneath this marma, while axillary artery, ulnar artery, median nerve and medial brachial cutaneous nerve in upper extremity.

**INDICATIONS:** *Tatra lohitkshayen maranam pakshaghato va*

तत्र लोहितक्षयेण मरणम पक्षाघातो वा

सु. शारीर 6/24

Haemoptysis (*urdhva raktapitta*) and uterine bleeding (*Adhoga raktapitta*), *pakshaghat* (Hemiplegia, paraplegia).

## LOHITAKSHA MARMA CHIKITSA

For above said ailments, following are the methods of stimulation:

1. **VIMLAPAN (Pressure):** Press the lohitaksha marma with middle finger.
2. **AGNIKARM:** Stimulation of marma by *dhoop* stick or moxa stick.In lower extremity femoral artery and vein is underneath this marma, while axillary artery, ulnar artery, median nerve and medial brachial cutaneous nerve in upper extremity.

# URVI MARMA

The meaning of uru is thigh and urvi is the marma of thigh. These are 4 in number, one in each limb. Two urvi marmas in upper extremity which are rightly named as Bahvi by *Astanghridayakar* (the word bahu is used for upper extremity).

**LOCATION:** According to Sushrut Sharir 6/24

*Urumadhye urvi tatra shonitkshayat sakthishoshah.*

उरुमध्ये उर्वी तत्र शोणितक्षयात् सक्थिशोषः

सु. शारीर 6/24

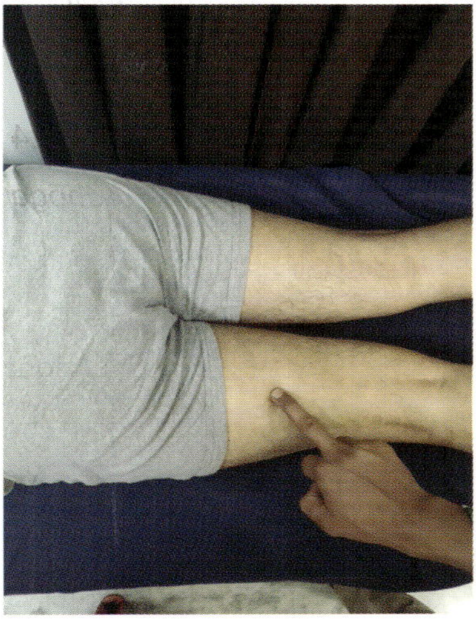

This sira marma lies in the middle of thigh and is of 1 *angul* size (2.0 to 3.0 cm), having *somya* and *agneya* quality. It comes under Vaikalyakar Marma. Due to affliction of this marma, loss of function of affected part takes place. Deficiency of blood causes atrophy of muscles of the extremities.

**RESPONSIBLE SIRA BINDU** (Meridian points): Sira of Mutrashay Dhamani (UB37) on posterior side of thigh, while Sira of Talhridaya dhamani (P2) in upper extremity.

## INDICATIONS

**Lower extremity:** Muscular atrophy, motor impairment, pain and paralysis of lower extremities.

**Upper extremity:** Pain in upper arm. This marma is also useful for cardiomyopathy and cardiac pain.

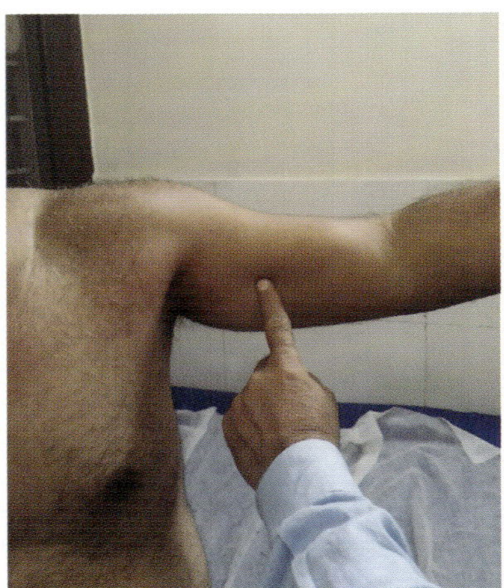

### URVI MARMA CHIKITSA

1. **VIMLAPAN (Pressure):** Press the above said marma point with the help of thumb or index finger.
2. **AGNIKARM (Moxibustion):** Moxibustion is also method of choice for Urvi marma.

# ANI MARMA

The meaning of Ani is the axle of wheel of bullock cart or tanga of older days. So if axle of a wheel is loosely fitted, there is wobbling of the wheel. The same is with affliction of Ani marma. Patient can't move due to numbness of foot. It is due to injury or tear of tendon. It is snayu marma and its size is half angul (1.0 to 1.5 cm).

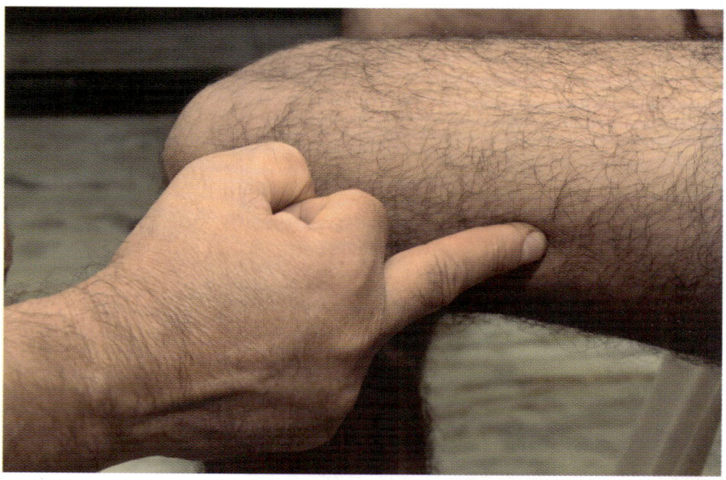

**LOCATION:** According to Sushrut Sharir 6/24

*Janun urdhvamubhayatastrayangulamani tatra shophabhivriddhih stabdhasakthita ch.*

जानुन ऊर्ध्वमुभयतस्त्रयंगुलमाणी तत्र शोफाभिवृद्धिः स्तब्धसक्थिता च।

सु. शारीर 6/24

Ani marma lies on either side, 3 fingers above the knee and elbow joints.It is vaikalyakar marma having *somya* as well as *agneya* property. On affliction of this marma, loss of function, swelling of knee and elbow joint and numbness of the extremities take place.

## RESPONSIBLE SIRA BINDU

**Lower extremity:** On lateral side sira of Pittashay and Amashay dhamani (GB31, St33)

On medial side Sira of Yakrit and Pliha dhamani (Liv9, Sp 10)

**Upper Extremity:** Dorsal side: Sira of Vrihadantra and Shleshmashay dhamani (LI12, Sj11)

**On ventral side:** Sira of Phuffus dhamani (Lu4)

**INDICATION:** Motor impairment of upper and lower extremity, numbness, pedal oedema, hemiplegia.

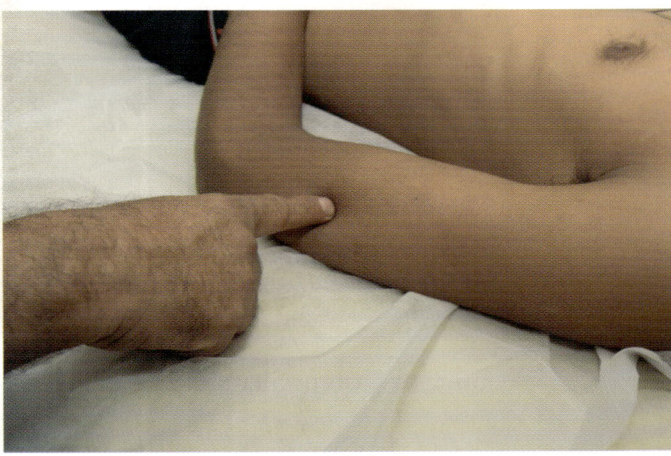

## ANI MARMA CHIKITSA

1. **VIMLAPAN:** Marmas of both sides should be stimulated by pressure. For better results, press with the help of all fingers.
2. **SIRAVEDHAN (puncture):** Puncture the above said points perpendicularly in 1.0 inch depth in lower extremity and ¼ to ½ inch depth in upper extremity.
3. **AGNIKARMA:** Pottali swed, Ekangdhara with Dhanvantar taila and Mahanarayan taila is beneficial.

## VITAP MARMA

Meaning of vitap is the septum of scrotum related with sex and spermatogenesis. This marma has its speciality because this is the marma of man exclusively. This marma is of *snayu* marma variety and present in upper most part of lower extremity.

**LOCATION:** According to Sushrut sharir 6/24

*Vankshanvrishanayorantare vitapam*
*Tatra shandhyamalpashukrata va bhavati.*

वंक्षणवृषणयोरंतरे विटपम तत्र षांढ्यमल्पशुक्रता वा भवति।

सु. शारीर 6/24

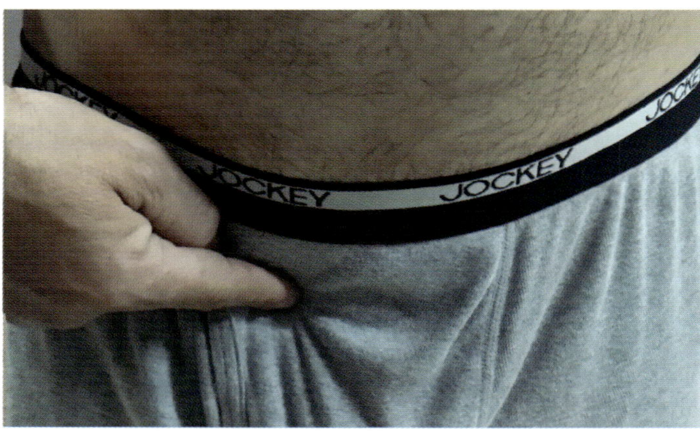


The vitap marma lies in between the scrotum and inguinal canal. Affliction of this marma causes impotency and oligospermia. This vaikalyakar marma is having s*omya* and a*gneya* quality and is one *angul* in size.

**RESPONSIBLE SIRA BINDU (Meridian points):** Sira of Vrikka dhamani (K 11) and sira of Artav nadi (Ren2) on the superior border of symphysis pubis.

**INDICATION:** Impotency and oligospermia (Shandhyam, Alpashukrata)

## VITAP MARM CHIKITSA

1. VIMLAPAN: Pressure with side movement or round movement with the help of middle finger or with four fingers.
2. AGNIKARM (Moxibustion): *Agnikarm* with the help of *dhoop* stick or moxa stick is beneficial.

# KAKSHADHAR MARMA

*Kaksha* means Axilla and *dhar* means holding, so meaning of kakshadhar is which holds the axilla. This marma lies in between chest and axillary pit. Affliction of this marma causes hemiplegia. This marma is of snayu marma variety and as per prognosis this is vaikalyakar marma having one *angul* size (2.0 cm-3.0 cm).

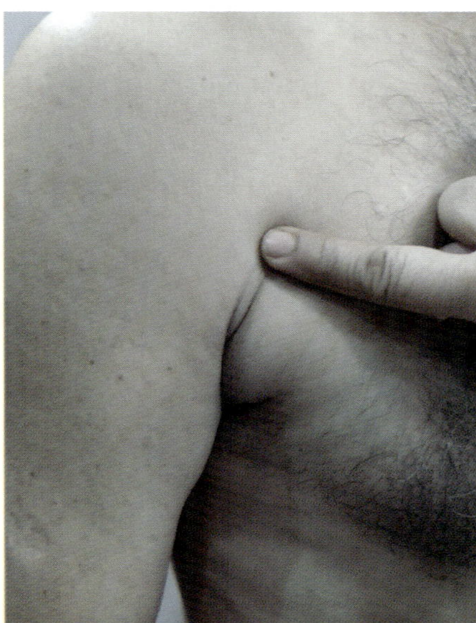

LOCATION: According to *Sushrut Sharir 6/24*

*Vakshah kakshayormadhye kakshadharam*

वक्ष:कक्षयोर्मध्ये कक्षधरं

सु. शारीर 6/24

**RESPONSIBLE SIRA BINDU (meridian points):** Extraordinary point of Chinese midway between the end of the anterior axillary fold and chest simulates with Sushruta's kakshadhar marma.

(Besides this, Sira of Shleshmashay dhamani (Sj 14) between acromian end of clavicle and greater tuberosity of humerous has same indications).

**INDICATION:** *kakshadhare pakshaghatah*

कक्षधरे पक्षाघातः

Hemiplegia and pain in the shoulder and arm.

### *KAKSHADHAR MARMA CHIKITSA*

1. **VIMLAPAN:** Press the marma with Index finger in rotatory movement.
2. **AGNIKARM:** Heating of marma point with the help of *dhoop* stick or moxa stick.

## KURCH MARMA

Kurch marmas are the marmas of hands (back of palm) and feet. These are four in number and are of snayu marma variety. Structurally these are brush or bundle like (*kurch* means brush). These marmas lie on the foot and hand just above the kshipra marma on both sides. These are Vaikalyakar marmas. Their size is 6.0 to 7.0 cm (*svapanital kunchit sammit*). On affliction of these marmas, there is defect or incompetency of hands and feet. There is shaking in hands and feet. It occurs only during walk or handling the work. Tremors occur only below the wrist and ankles.

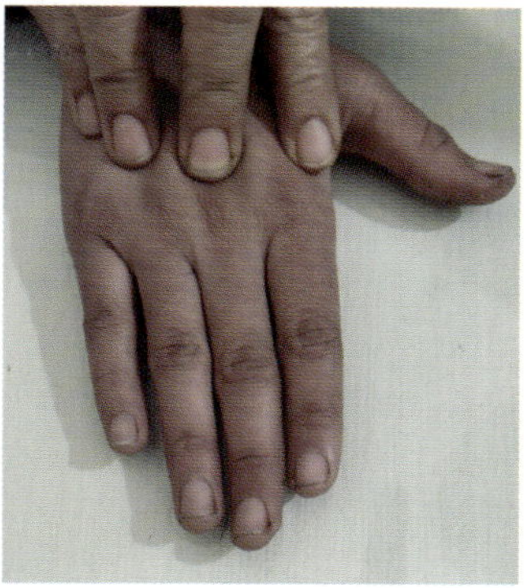

According to *Sushrut sharir 6/24:*

*Kshiprasyoparishtadubhayatah kurcho naam, padasya bhramanvepane bhavatah.*

क्षिप्रस्योपरिष्टादुभयतः कूर्चो नाम, पादस्य भ्रमणवेपने भवतः।

सुश्रुत शारीर 6/24

## RESPONSIBLE SIRA BINDU

**Upper extremity:** Sira of Laghvantra Dhamani and Shleshmashay Dhamani (SI2, SI3, SJ2, SJ3, LI3)

**Lower Extremity:** Sira of Pittashay and Amashay Dhamani (GB41, GB42, GB43, ST43)

**INDICATIONS:** These marmas lie on the dorsum of foot and hand. Have their indication for incompetency of hands and feet due to pain and motor impairment.

## KURCH MARMA CHIKITSA

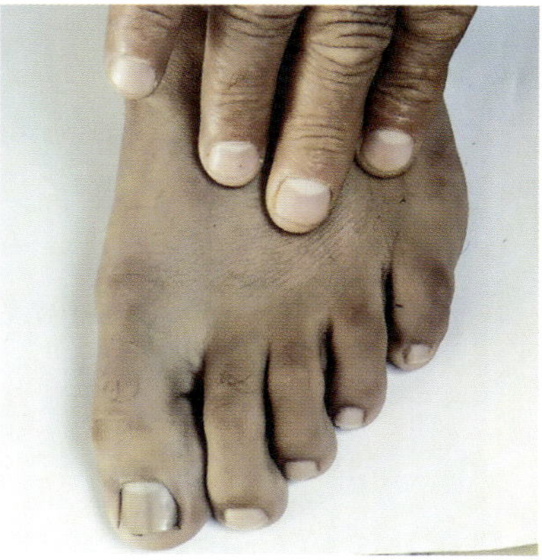

1. **VIMLAPAN:** Press the marma points with the help of all four fingers or with thumb of both hands.
2. **AGNIKARM:** Heat the above said marma points with *dhoop* stick or moxa.
3. **SIRAVEDHAN:** Puncture the above said points.

# KURCHSHIR MARMA

As *Kurch* means brush, Kurchshir denotes head of brush where all the fibres of brush unite and make a thick bundle. These are also of snayu marma variety and are the marmas of extremities. These marmas lie on either sides just below the Gulph sandhi in lower extremity and Manibandh sandhi in upper extremity. On affliction of this marma, pain and inflammation occurs. Cardinal features of snayu marma affliction are tremors, numbness, pain and convulsions. These are Rujakar marmas and have *Agni* and *Vayu tatva* and one *angul* in size (2.0-3.0 cm).

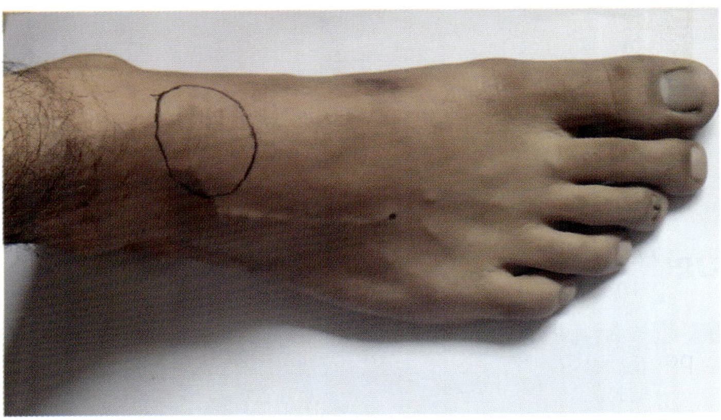

**INDICATIONS:** Pain and inflammation of whole body and of dorsum of hand and feet.

According to *Sushrut sharir 6/24*

*Gulphsandheradh ubhyatah kurchshirah, tatra rujashophou*

गुल्फसंधेरध उभयतः कूर्चशिरः, तत्र रुजाशोफौ

सुश्रुत शारीर 6/24

## RESPONSIBLE SIRA BINDU

**In lower extremity:** Sira of Pittashay and Amashay Dhamani (GB40 and St 41)

**In upper extremity:** Sira of Shleshmashay and Laghvantra dhamani (Sj 4 and SI 4).

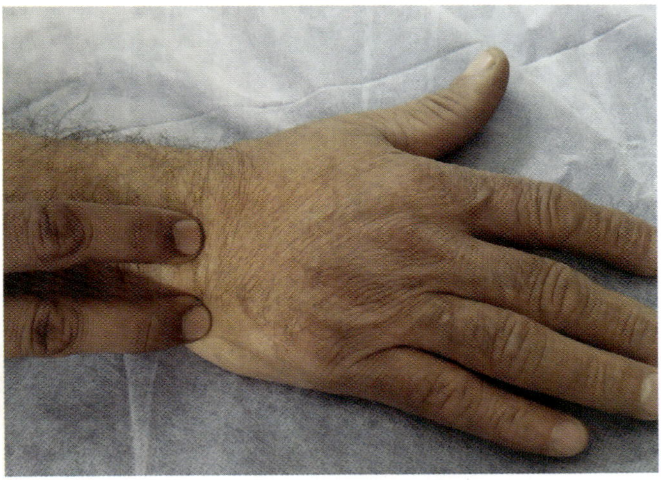

## *KURCHSHIR MARMA CHIKITSA*

1. **VIMLAPAN:** Pressure is applied on the above said marma points with the help of thumb or index finger.
2. **AGNIKARM:** Heating the marma points with the help of moxa or *dhoop* stick also gives very good results.
3. **SIRAVEDHAN:** Puncture the above said marma points.

## VASTI MARMA

Vasti marma is an important marma of abdomen and pelvic cavity. It is one in number and is of *snayu marma* variety. Its size is 6.0 to 7.0 cm (*svapanital kunchit sammit*). This is *agneya marma* i.e. fire element is predominant. Acharya Charak has given it due importance by placing it in *Trimarmeeya* group (very important 3 marmas i.e. Shir, Hridaya and Vasti). This is sadya pranhar marma.

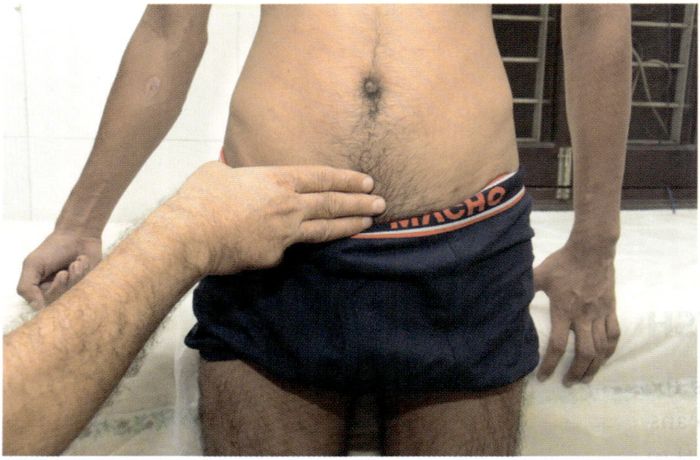


**LOCATION:** According to Sushrut Samhita sharir sthan 6/25

*Alpamansshonitamabhyantartah katyam mutrashayo vastih,*
*tatrapi sadyomarnam.*

अल्पमांसशोणितामभ्यंतरतः कट्यां मूत्राशयो वस्तिः, तत्रापि सद्योमरणं

सु. शारीर 6/25

**RESPONSIBLE SIRA BINDU (Meridian points):** Point on Artav nadi (Ren 3, 4, 5, 6)

**INDICATIONS:** This marma affects complete urogenital system. Being *snayu* marma, it is also responsible for stroke (flaccid type of apoplexy). This marma has its indication for oedema, urinary incontinence, uterine bleeding, irregular menstruation, abdominal pain and renal colic.

### *VASTI MARMA CHIKITSA*

1. VIMLAPAN: Press the marma point by pinching method.
2. AGNIKARM: Fomentation by hot water bag. The same effect can be taken by heating the above said points (moxibustion).

NOTE : According to Chinese accupuncture Ren 3 is front-Mu point while UB28 is back-Su point of Urinary bladder.

## KSHIPRA MARMA

As the name indicates, this is a very fast acting marma (*kshipra* means quick). These are four in number having half *angul* size (1.0 to 1.5 cm).

LOCATION: According to *Sushrut Sharir 6/24*

*Tatra padasyangushthangulyormadhye kshipram naam marma,*
*Tatraviddhasyaakshepken maranam.*

तत्र पादस्यांगुष्ठांगुल्योरमध्ये क्षिप्रं नाम मर्म, तत्रविद्धस्याक्षेपकेन मरणं

सु. शारीर 6/24

It lies between the metacarpal of thumb and index finger in the upper extremity. In lower extremity it lies in between metatarsal of big toe and the adjacent finger. Kshipra marma is the marma of blood coagulating system as well as *Akshep* (Apoplexy, convulsions and epilepsy). When this marma is afflicted, there is haemorrhage because of defective blood coagulating system resulting in haemoptysis, haematemesis, epistaxis, uterine bleeding etc. As haemorrhage deteriorates vayu, apoplexy takes place and patient falls like a rooted out tree. As this is kalantar pranhar marma, the patient dies after long duration.

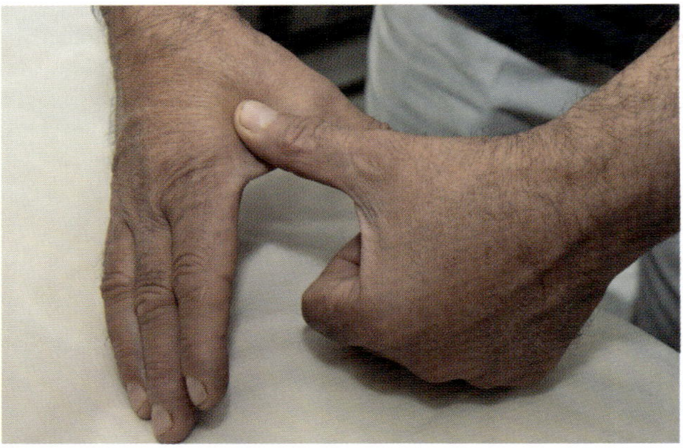

## RESPONSIBLE SIRA BINDU (Meridian points)

**Upper extremity:** Sira of Vrihadantra dhamani (LI 4) between first and second metacarpal bones.

**Lower extremity:** Sira of Yakrit dhamani (Liv 2, 3) situated in between first and second metatarsal bones.

**INDICATION:** In Sushrut Samhita Sharir Sthan 6/24 Acharya Sushrut says

*'Tatraviddhasya akshepken maranam'*

तत्र विद्धस्य आक्षेपकेन मरणं

सु. शारीर 6/24

Here we want to make it clear that patient will not die due to injury of its vital point (kshipra marma) which is present in hands and feet. Instead, blood coagulating Kshipra marma system of body will be affected by disease and patient will die due to *akshep* (apoplexy) and this problem can be treated by its vital marma points present in extremities.

## KSHIPRA MARMA CHIKITSA

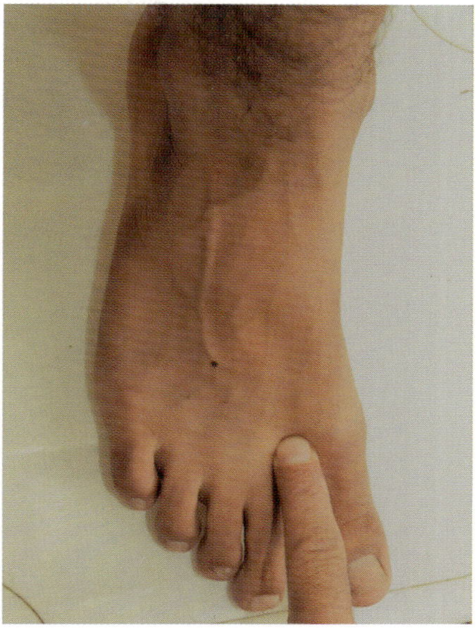

Above said vital points should be stimulated for its indications of pain, bleeding disorders, apoplexy and convulsions. Following are the methods to be used:

1. VIMLAPAN: Marma should be stimulated by pressing the point with the help of thumb. For heavy stimulation pressure should be applied by rotatory movement of thumb depending on the tolerance of that particular person.
2. AGNIKARM: *Agnikarm* by moxa or *dhoop* stick is beneficial.
3. SIRAVEDHAN: Puncture the above said sira bindu 0.5 to 1cm deep.

## ANS MARMA

Ans marma is related to numbness and motor impairment of hand *(tatra stabdha bahuta)*. It comes under the category of Vaikalyakar marma and is of *snayu marma* variety. Its size is half *angul* (1.0 to 1.5 cm) and is of *somya* as well as *agneya* quality.

**LOCATION:** According to Sushrut Sharir 6/26

*Bahumurdhagreevamadhye anspeeth skandhbandhanavansou, tatra stabdhbahuta.*

बाहुमूर्धग्रीवामध्ये अंसपीठ स्कन्धबंधनावंसौ, तत्र स्तब्धबाहुता

सु. शारीर 6/26

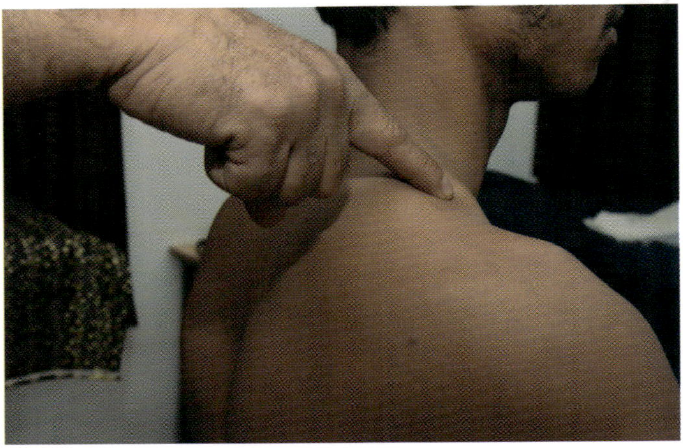

This marma lies in between the shoulder and neck. The muscles and *snayu tantra* which bind the shoulder, scapula and acromial end of clavicle with head of humerous take part to make the outer supportive structures of Ans marma.

**INDICATIONS:** Ans marma has its main indication for numbness and motor impairment of hand.

**RESPONSIBLE SIRA BINDU (MERIDIAN POINTS):** Sira of Pittashay dhamani (GB21)

## ANS MARMA CHIKITSA

For above said indications, following are the methods to be used:

1. **VIMLAPAN:** Ans marma can be stimulated by applying pressure of thumb. Pressure of 10 times round movements of thumb should be applied on marma. For mild stimulation,

marma should be stimulated by applying pressure of middle finger while for heavy stimulation, pressure with the help of all four fingers or by pinching with thumb and four fingers gives better results.

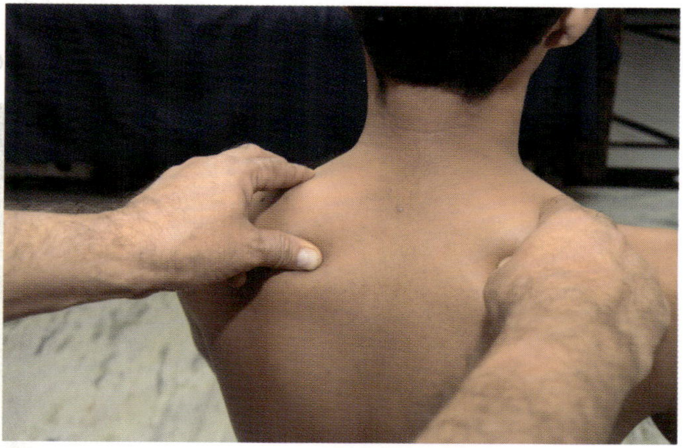

2. **AGNIKARM:** *Agnikarm* by moxa stick or *dhoop* stick is beneficial. *Pottali swed* of Ans marma including Ansaphalak marma is beneficial.
3. **SIRAVEDHAN:** Puncturing of above said *sira bindu* is another method.

Along with Ans marma, **Ansphalak marma** is used for the treatment of *Ansgat vata* (Cervical spondylosis).

## UTKSHEP MARMA

Utkshep marma is the marma of head and is of vishalyaghna marma variety hence needs continuous treatment.

*Shankhayorupari keshant utkshepou, tatra sashalyo jeevet pakat patitshalyo va noddhritshalyah.*

*Sushrut Sharir 6/27*

शंखयोरूपरि केशान्त उत्क्षेपौ, तत्र सशल्यो जीवेत् पाकात् पतितशल्यो वा नोद्धृतशल्यः।

सु. शारीर 6/27

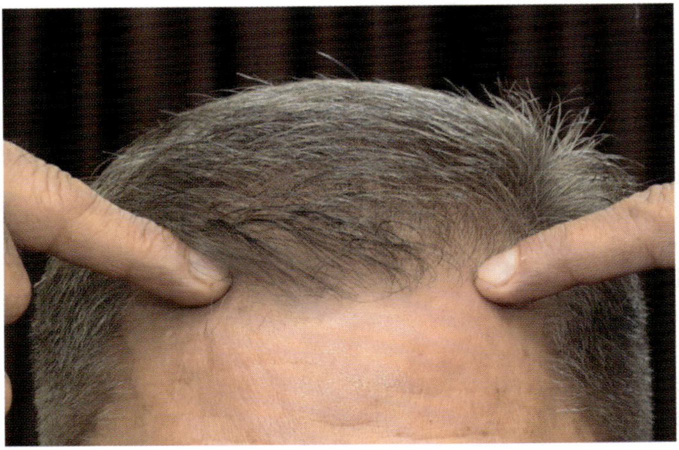

According to Acharya Sushrut, this marma lies on the upper most part of the forehead over the hairline and above the Shankh marma. This marma comes under snayu marma and prognosis wise it is Yapya marma, so needs continuous treatment for survival. Its size is half *angul* (1.0 to 1.5cm).

**RESPONSIBLE SIRA BINDU (MERIDIAN POINTS):** It may be extra channel point near sira of Amashay dhamani (St 8).

**INDICATIONS:** Epilepsy, mental disorders, infantile convulsions, vertigo

## UTKSHEP MARMA CHIKITSA

For these indications, above said marma bindu should be stimulated.

1. VIMLAPAN: *Vimlapan* (pressure massage) is method of choice.
2. AGNIKARM: Heat the above said point with the help of *dhoop* or moxa stick.

# VIDHUR MARMA

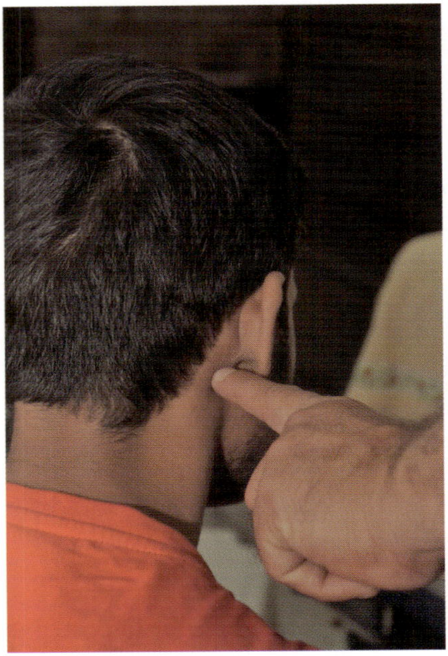

Vidhur marma is related with *Badhiryam* (deafness). This urdhvajatru marma is half *angul* (1.0 to 1.5 cm) in size and is of *snayu* marma variety. This marma lies on the lower side of the root of the ear on the posterior and inferior border of the mastoid process in the depression between the mandible and mastoid process.

LOCATION: According to *Sushrut Samhita sharir sthan 6/27*

*Karnaprishthatoadhah sanshrite vidhure, tatra badhiryam*

कर्णपृष्ठतोअध: संश्रिते विधुरे, तत्र बाधिर्य

सु. शारीर 6/27

This marma is the marma of deafness. According to Acharya Sushrut, when vitiated vayu alone or mixed with kaph surrounds the auditory centres and gets fixed, it causes immediate deafness (damage of vestibulo cochlear nerve causes deafness or ringing in the ears). Vitiated vayu reaching the internal sense organs destroys its functions, causing deafness.

**RESPONSIBLE SIRA BINDU (Meridian points):** Sira of Shleshmashay dhamani (Sj 16,17)

**INDICATIONS:** Tinnitus, deafness.

*Tatra badhiryam*

*Sushrut Sharir 6/27*

तत्र बाधिर्य

सु. शारीर 6/27

## VIDHUR MARMA CHIKITSA

1. **VIMLAPAN:** Press the marma point with the help of index finger or thumb.
2. **AGNIKARM:** Heat the above said point with the help of *dhoop* stick or moxa stick.

## KATIKTARUN MARMA

Katiktarun marma is kalantar pranhar marma (death after some time due to pain and loss of blood). This asthi marma is the marma of lower back.

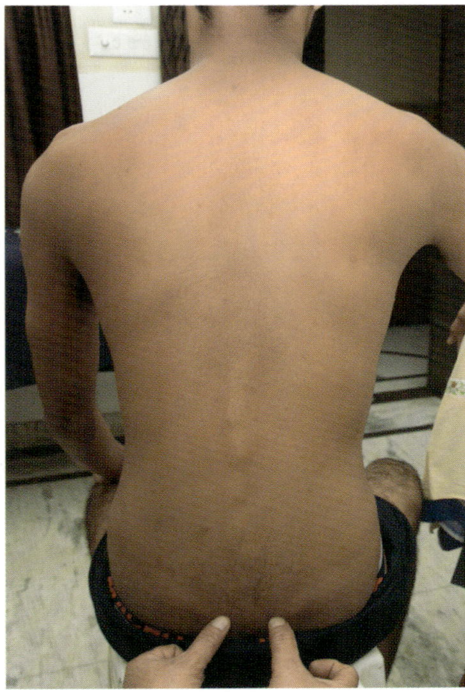

Due to affliction of this marma, there is severe shooting and piercing pain. Patient becomes anaemic, colourless and dusty.

According to *Sushrut Samhita Sutra sthan 25/39* severe pain occurs due to affliction of asthi marma.

*Ghorarujo yasya nishadineshu sarvasvavasthasu na shantirasti,*
*Trishnangasadou shvayathushch ruk ch Tamasthividdham manujam vyavasyet.*

घोरारुजो यस्य निशादिनेषु सर्वास्ववस्थासु न शान्तिरस्ति
तृष्णाअंगसादौ श्वयथुश्च रुक् च तमस्थिविद्धं मनुजं व्यवस्येत्

सु. सूत्र 25/39

This marma is of half angul size (1.0 to 1.5 cm).

**LOCATION:** According to *Sushrut Samhita Sharir Sthan 6/26*

*Tatra prishthvanshamubhayatah pratishronikandamasthini katiktarune, tatra shonitkshayat pandurvivarno heenroopashch mriyate.*

तत्रपृष्ठवंशमुभयतः प्रतिश्रोणिकाण्डमस्थिनी कटीकतरुणे,
तत्रशोणितक्षयात् पाण्डुर्विवर्णो हीनरूपश्च म्रियते

सु. शारीर 6/26

This marma lies in the bones of ***shronikand*** (sacral bones) and in both sides of lower end of vertebral column *(Prishthavanshamubhayatah).*

## RESPONSIBLE SIRA BINDU

Sira of Mutrashay dhamani (UB31, UB32, UB53) both sides on first and second posterior sacral foramina.

INDICATIONS: Severe pain over lumbosacral area. Severe anaemia due to haemorrhoids, uterine bleeding.

## *KATIKTARUN MARMA CHIKITSA*

1. VIMLAPAN: For above said ailments, *vimlapan* (massage with pressure) is the easy method.
2. AGNIKARM: *Agnikarm* by moxa stick or *dhoop* stick is beneficial. Patient suffering from acute low back pain can be relieved by performing pottali swed.
3. SIRAVEDHAN (Puncture): Puncture perpendicularly above said points to the depth of 0.7 to 1.0 inch.

# NITAMB MARMA

Nitamb marma is the kalantar pranhar asthi marma of back. According to Sushrut Sharir 6/26

*Shronikandayoruparyashayachchadanou parshvantarpratibaddhou Nitambou.*

श्रोणिकाण्डयोरूपर्याशयाच्छादनौ पार्श्वांतरप्रतिबद्धौ नितम्बौ।

सुश्रुत शारीर 6/26

Its size is half *angul* (1.0 cm to 1.5 cm). When this marma is afflicted, there is atrophy of muscles of lower extremities leading to impairment of functions of lower part of the body with general debility.

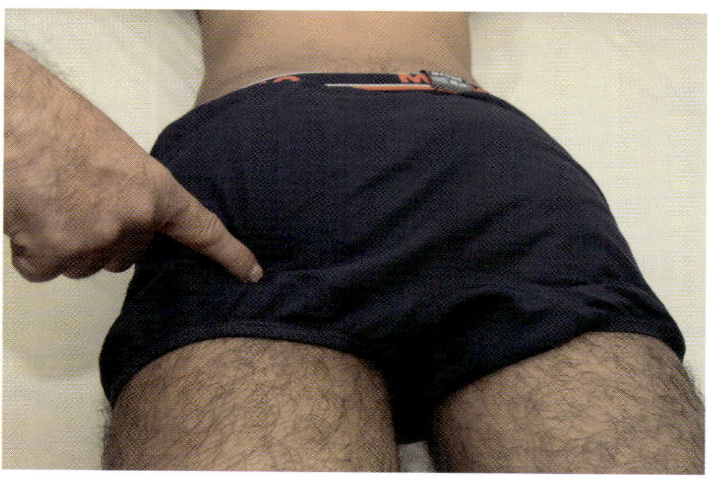

**RESPONSIBLE SIRA BINDU :** Sira of pittashay dhamani (GB 30) which is in between greater and lesser trochanter.

**INDICATIONS :** *Tatradhah kaya shosho dourbalyachch maranam.*

*Sushrut sharir 6/26*

तत्राधः कायशोषो दौर्बल्याच्च मरणं

सु. शारीर 6/26

Hemiplegia, atrophy of muscles of lower extremities, low backache, pain in lower extremities, lumbago sciatica syndrome, prolapsed intervertebral disc.

## NITAMB MARMA CHIKITSA

For above said indications following are the methods:

1. **VIMLAPAN :** Press the marma with the help of middle finger or with all four fingers simultaneously.
2. **SIRAVEDHAN :** Puncture 4 to 5 cm deep with the help of needle.

## ANSPHALAK MARMA

Ansphalak marma is also kalantar pranhar asthi marma of upper back. This marma is half *angul* (1.0-1.5 cm) in size. On upper back ansphalak marma lies on both sides of vertebral column between spinous process of Ist and IInd thoracic vertebra and medial border of scapula on either side. The word Phalak is used for broad flat bones. Both sides of scapula and thoracic vertebra collectively form TRIK-joining of three structures.

*prishthvanshmubhayatastriksambaddhe ansphalake*

*Su. Sharir 6/26*

पृष्ठवंशमुभयतस्त्रिकसम्बद्धे अंसफलके

सु. शारीर 6/26

**RESPONSIBLE SIRA BINDU:** Sira of Mutrashay dhamani (UB 11 and 41) 3.5 cm lateral to the lower border of spinous process of the 1st Thoracic vertebra. The point UB 41 is just below and lateral to it.

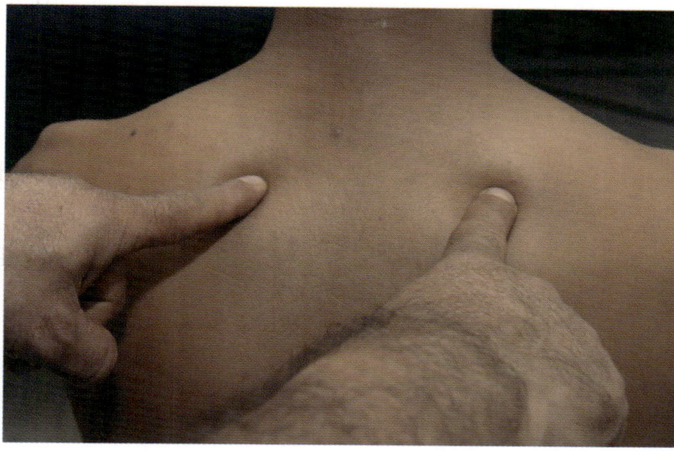

**INDICATIONS:** Arthritis and numbness of upper limbs, brachial neuritis, cervical spondylosis.

*Tatra Bahvoh swapshoshou.*

*Su .Sharir 6/26*

तत्र बाह्वोः स्वापशोषौ।

सुश्रुत शारीर 6/26

**ANSPHALAK MARMA CHIKITSA :** For above said indications, following are the methods:

1. **VIMLAPAN :** Press the marma with middle finger or with thumb. For best results, Ansphalak marma and Ans marma should be stimulated simultaneously by *vimlapan* method. (Press with rotatory movement)
2. **AGNIKARM :** *Agnikarm* with the help of *Dhoop* stick or moxa. Heating the marma area with the help of pottali (Pottali swed) is beneficial.

3. **SIRAVEDHAN :** Puncture the above said sira bindu 0.5 inch obliquely.

## SHANKH MARMA

Shankh marma is sadhya pranhar agneya asthi marma of *urdhvajatru* (above clavicle). Size of this marma is half *angul* (1.0 to 1.5 cm). This marma is not in regular channels but it belongs to extra channel.

**LOCATION:** According to Sushrut sharir 6/27

*Bhruvorantayorupari karnalalatayormadhye shankhou, tatra sadhyo maranam.*

भ्रुवोरंतयोरुपरि कर्णललाटयोर्मध्ये शंखौ, तत्र सद्यो मरणं

सु. शारीर 6/27

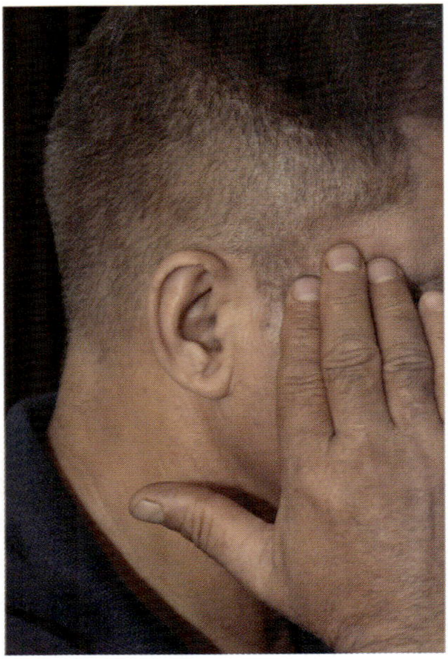

This marma lies on upper part of the end of eyebrow and the centre of the line drawn on the upper part of the ear lobule to the forehead. Utkshep is above this marma. So it is an area between Utkshep on the upper part and Apang marma below. This Temporal area is higly innervated by the sensory root of the Trigeminal nerve causing shock due to severe pain. Temporal artery is underneath this.

## JANU MARMA

The word Janu is used for knee. This marma lies between leg and thigh.

*Janghorvoh sandhane janu, tatra khanjata.*

*Sushrut sharir 6/24*

जङ्घोर्वोः संधाने जानु, तत्र खंजता।

सु. शारीर 6/24

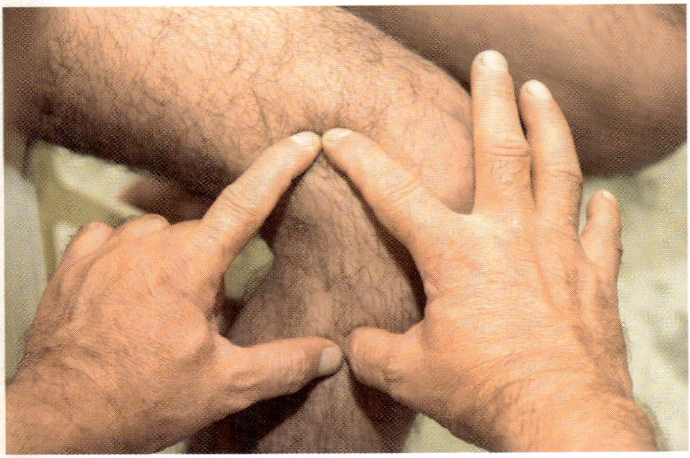

This is Vaikalyakar Sandhi marma. This marma is *somya* as well as *agneya* having three *angul* size (6.0 cm to 9.0 cm). Affliction of this marma causes lameness.

**RESPONSIBLE SIRA BINDU:** Sira bindu of Pittashay, Mutrashay and Amashay Dhamani (GB32, GB34, UB40, St34, St35)

**INDICATIONS:** Pain of Knee joint, hemiplegia, motor impairment of lower extremity.

### JANU MARMA CHIKITSA

1. **VIMLAPAN :** *Vimlapan* of Janu marma sira bindu reduces the problem.
2. **AGNIKARM :** *Agnikarma* is also the method of choice for its stimulation.

   Janu vasti, Patra pinda pottali sved or Nadi sved after vathar oil massage reduces the pain and inflammation.
3. **SIRAVEDHAN:** Puncture the above said Janu marma points.

**NOTE:** If we consider Janu marma on medial side the points will be K 10, Liv7, Liv8, Sp9, Sp10

## KURPAR MARMA

This sandhi marma of upper extremity is Vaikalyakar marma and is of three *angul* size (6.0 cm to 9.0 cm). This marma is responsible for pain of elbow and arm, and motor impairment of upper extremity.

According to Sushrut Sharir 6/24

*Yani sakthini gulphjanuvitapani tani bahou manibandhkurpar kakshdharani*

यानि सक्थिनि गुल्फजानुविटपानि तानि बाहौ मणिबंधकूर्पर कक्षधराणि

सु. शारीर 6/24

**RESPONSIBLE SIRA BINDU:** Sira of Vrihadantra, Shleshmashay and Laghvantra Dhamani (LI11, Sj10 and SI8)

**INDICATIONS:** According to *Sushrut Sharir 6/24*

*Kurparakhye kunih.*

कूर्पराख्ये कुणिः।

सुश्रुत शारीर 6/24

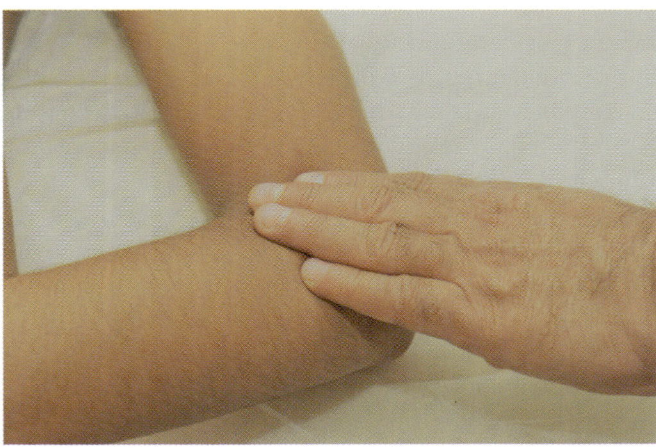

## KURPAR MARMA CHIKITSA

Kurpar marma is most vulnerable marma for sports injuries. It is a very effective marma for treating Tennis elbow. Methods for stimulation of Kurpar marma are:

1. **VIMLAPAN:** Because of its big area, this marma can be

stimulated with the help of all four fingers on one side while thumb on another side.

2. **AGNIKARM:** *Agnikarm* by *Dhoop* stick or moxa stick. Pottali swed, Ekangdhara, Nadi swed can also be performed.
3. **SIRAVEDHAN:** *Siravedh* (Needling) on above said sira bindu works very effectively.

## SIMANT MARMA

This sandhi marma of urdhvajatru (above the clavicle) lies at the junction of five sutures of skull bones. Having the size of 6.0 to 7.0 cm (*svapanital kunchit sammit*), this is kalantar pranhar marma (death after some time) and is of *somya* as well as *agneya* property. According to Acharya Sushrut

*Panch Sandhayah shirasi vibhaktah simanta naam,*
*tatronmad bhaya chittanashairmaranam*

*Sushrut Sharir 6/27*

पंचसंधयः शिरसि विभक्ताः सीमंता नाम, तत्रोन्मादभयचित्तनाशैर्मरणम

सुश्रुत शारीर 6/27

On affliction of this marma *Unmad* (madness), *Bhaya* (fear complex), *Chittanash* (loss of memory, intelligence, reasoning and loss of consciousness) like symptoms develop and ultimately lead to death after a long duration.

## RESPONSIBLE SIRA BINDU

Extraordinary point "Sishencong" of Chinese literature covers the definition of Simant marma, which corresponds to one finger posterior, anterior and lateral to the Adhipati marma.

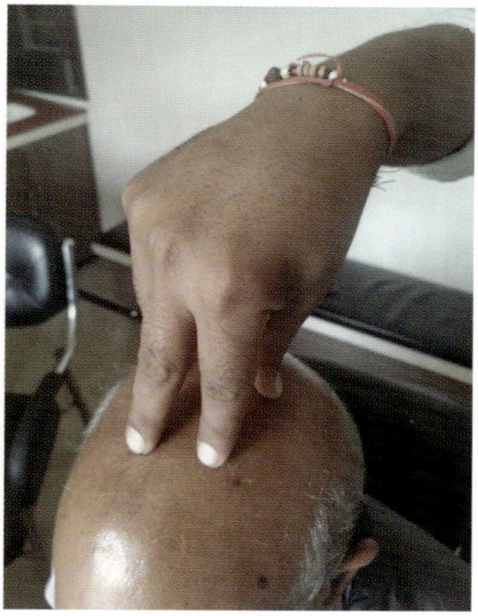

**INDICATIONS:** Epilepsy (*Apasmar*), Madness (*unmad*), fear complex, Anxiety, Loss of memory.

### *SIMANT MARMA CHIKITSA*

For above said indications, Simant marma should be stimulated by following methods:

1. **VIMLAPAN:** Simant marma area should be rubbed mildly by using shatdhout ghrit.
2. **AGNIKARM:** Mild heating with the help of *dhoop* stick or moxa stick.

**NOTE:** In Sushrut Samhita Kalp Sthan Chapter 5/23, Acharya Sushrut indicated this marma for snake bite.

## ADHIPATI MARMA

Adhipati marma is the governing centre of all dhamanis and marmas; therefore it is known as Adhipati. This is the marma of head. This marma lies on the top of centre of vertex at the junctions of siras and joints of skull bones.

According to Sushrut Sharir 6/27

*Mastakabhyantaroparishtat sira sandhi sannipato romavarto adhipatih.*

मस्तकाभ्यंतरोपरिष्टात् सिरासंधिसन्निपातो रोमावर्तो अधिपतिः।

सुश्रुत शारीर 6/27

Jointly with Simant marma, it can be used for epilepsy, apoplexy, Schizophrenia, Parkinsonism and mental disorders. This meeting point of several points is the Baihui point of Chinese. Having *agneya* quality and half *angul* size (1.0 to 1.5 cm), this sandhi marm is sadhya pranhar marma.

**RESPONSIBLE SIRA BINDU:** Shukra nadi (Du 20) on the mid point of the line connecting the apexes of the two auricles.

**INDICATIONS:** Mental disorders, sleeplessness and anxiety.

**ADHIPATI MARMA CHIKITSA:** Adhipati marma should be stimulated with Simant marma. Following are the methods for stimulation of Adhipati marma:

1. **VIMLAPAN:** Shatdhout ghrit should be rubbed on Adhipati marma by gentle massage, or marma can be stimulated by

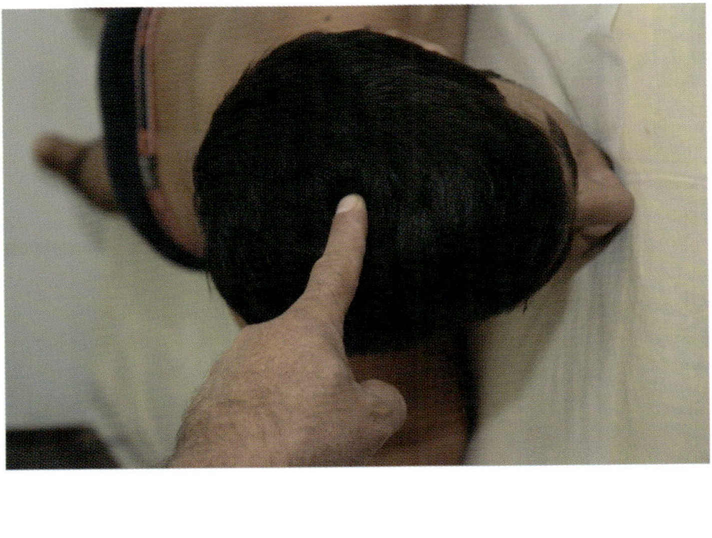

applying gentle pressure with the help of middle or index finger.

2. AGNIKARM: Mild heating on Adhipati marma sira bindu with the help of ***dhoop*** stick or moxa. Direct heating or scarification can be performed by highly experienced physician.

## GULPH MARMA

Gulph marma is the sandhi marma of lower extremity related to ankle joint. This marma has two ***angul*** (4.0 to 6.0 cm) size and is of rujakar marma variety.

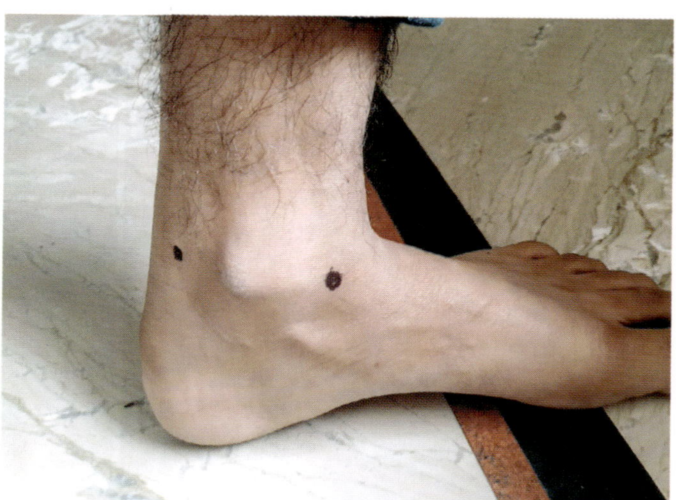

According to Sushrut Sharir 6/24

*Padjanghayoh sandhane gulphah*

पादजंघयोः संधाने गुल्फः

सु. शारीर 6/24

This marma lies at the junction of foot and leg. It is indicated for pain, numbness and limping.

**RESPONSIBLE SIRA BINDU:** Sira of Pittashay dhamani and Mutrashay dhamani (GB 39 and UB 59)

Other possibilities

(a) K3, Sp5

(b) K4, UB60

**INDICATIONS:** This marma is related to pain, numbness, weakness, paralysis of foot and hemiplegia. According to Sushrut Sharir 6/24

*Tatra rujah stabdhpadata khanjata va.*

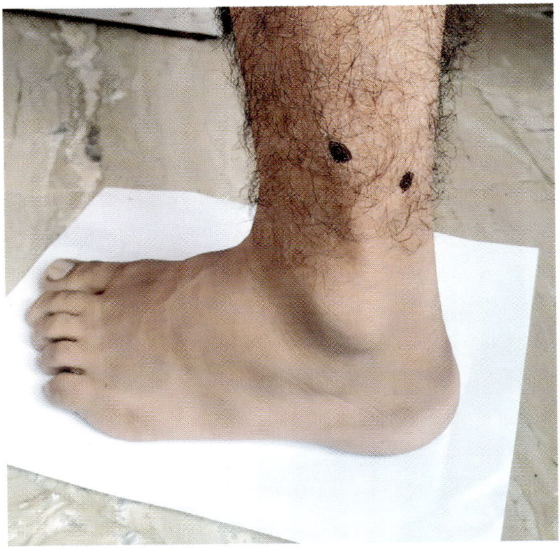

तत्र रुजः स्तब्धपादता खंजता वा

सु. शारीर 6/24

## GULPH MARMA CHIKITSA

For above said ailments, Gulph marma chikitsa should be performed as follows:

1. **VIMLAPAN:** Above said sira bindu should be stimulated by *vimlapan* method.
2. **AGNIKARM:** Mild heating with the help of *dhoop* stick or moxa gives quick and satisfactory relief.
3. **SIRAVEDHAN:** Puncture the above said sira bindu.

# MANIBANDH MARMA

According to Sushrut Sharir 6/24

*Yani sakthini gulphjanuvitapani tani bahou manibandh kurparkakshdharani*

यानि सक्थिनि गुल्फजानुविटपानि तानि बाहौ मणिबंधकूर्पर कक्षधराणि

सु. शारीर 6/24

This sandhi marma of upper extremity is of two *angul* size (4.0 to 6.0 cm). This is rujakar marma having its location on the wrist at the junction of hand and forearm.

**RESPONSIBLE SIRA BINDU:** Sira of laghvantra and Shleshmashay dhamani (SI 5 and Sj5)

**INDICATIONS:** *Manibandhe Kunthata* Su. Sharir 6/24

मणिबन्धे कुंठता

सु. शारीर 6/24

Impaired and loss of function of wrist, elbow and arm. This is also indicated for contraction and pain of elbow and arm.

## MANIBANDH MARMA CHIKITSA

1. VIMLAPAN (PRESSURE): Stimulate Manibandh marma by *vimlapan* method.
2. AGNIKARMA: Mild heating with the help of *dhoop* stick or moxa or *patra pinda pottali swed* give quick relief.
3. SIRAVEDHAN: Puncture the above said sira bindu.

Other possibilities

(a) SI5, Sj5, LI5

(b) Lu9, P7

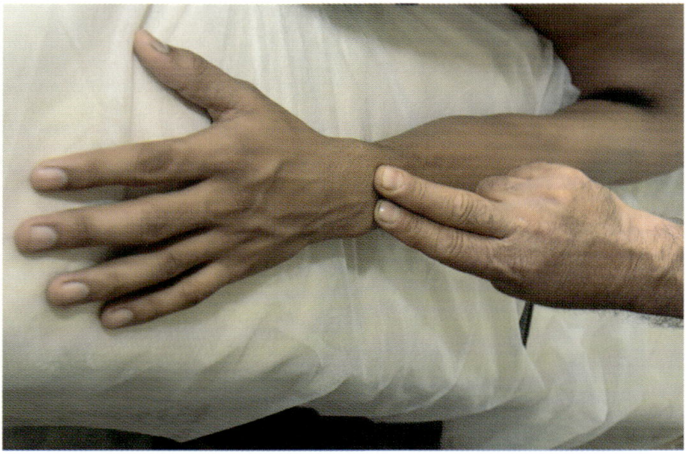

# KUKUNDAR MARMA

Kukundar marma is vaikalyakar marma (loss of function) and is of sandhi marma variety. Its size is half *angul* (1.0 to 1.5 cm). This marma lies on either side of lower part of vertebral column on the lateral and outer side of hip joint, in between the anterosuperior iliac spine and the greater trochanter.

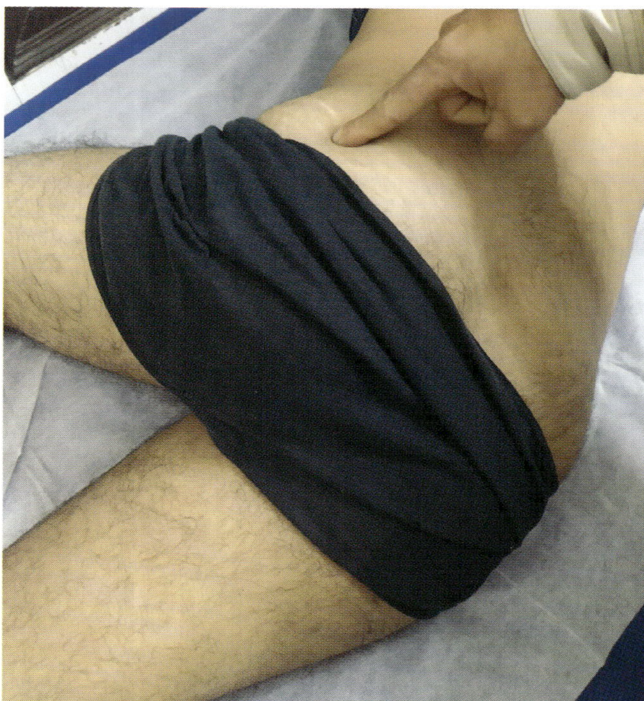

*Parshvayorjaghan bahirbhage prishthvanshamubhayato kukundare.*

*Sushrut sharir 6/26*

पार्श्वयोर्जघनबहिर्भागे पृष्ठवंशमुभयतो कुकुंदरे

सु. शारीर 6/26

On affliction of this marma, there is loss of sense of touch and impairment of function of the lower part of the body.

**RESPONSIBLE SIRA BINDU:** Sira of Pittashay dhamani (GB 29)

**INDICATIONS:** Loss of sense of touch and loss of function of lower part of the body. This condition occurs in sciatic nerve palsy and prolapsed intervertebral lumbar or lumbosacral disc.

*Tatra sparshagyanamadhahkaye cheshtopaghatashch*

*Su. Sharir 6/26*

तत्र स्पर्शज्ञानमधःकाये चेष्टोपघातश्च

सु. शारीर 6/26

### KUKUNDAR MARMA CHIKITSA

1. **VIMLAPAN (PRESSURE):** Stimulate Kukundar marma by *vimlapan* method.
2. **AGNIKARM:** The above said sira bindu should be stimulated with the help of *dhoop* stick or moxa. Pottali swed also gives good results.
3. **SIRAVEDH:** Puncture the above said sira bindu.

## AVART MARMA

Situated on both sides of forehead, this sandhi marma is vaikalyakar marma and is of somya as well as Agneya quality. This marma is having half angul size (1.0 to 1.5 cm). According to Sushrut Sharir Sthan 6/27

*Bhruvorupari nimnayoravarto naam.*

भ्रुवोरूपरिनिम्नयोरावर्तो नाम

सुश्रुत शारीर 6/27

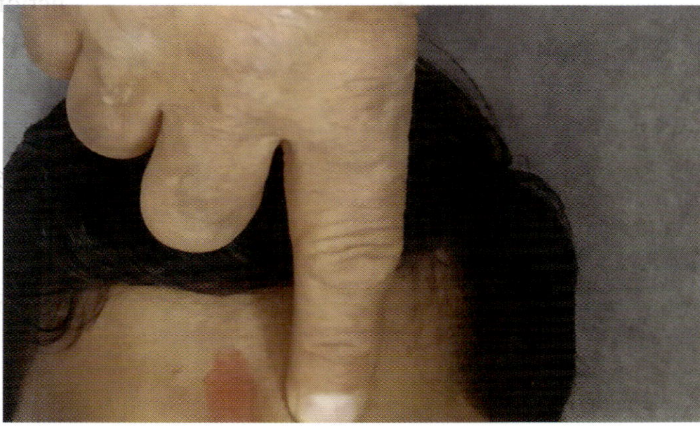

This marma lies just above the eyebrows on the lower part of the forehead.

**RESPONSIBLE SIRA BINDU:** Sira of Pittashay Dhamani (GB 14)

**INDICATIONS:** In Sushrut Samhita Sharir Sthan 6/27 Acharya Sushrut says,

*Tatrapyandhyam drishtyupghato va*

तत्राप्यान्ध्यं दृष्ट्युपघातो वा

सुश्रुत शारीर 6/27

This marma has its indication for blurring of vision.

## AVART MARMA CHIKITSA

For above said indications, following methods can be used:

1. **VIMLAPAN:** Press the marma point with the help of index or middle finger.

2. **AGNIKARM:** Mild heating of Avart marma with the help of *dhoop* or moxa stick.

## KRIKATIKA MARMA

This sandhi marma of urdhvajatru (above the clavicle) is vaikalyakar marma and has *somya* as well as *agneya* quality. The size of this marma is half *angul* (1.0 to 1.5 cm). In Sharir Sthan 6/27, Acharya Sushrut says:

*Shirogreevayoh sandhane krikatike.*

शिरोग्रीवयोः संधाने कृकाटिके

सुश्रुत शारीर 6/27

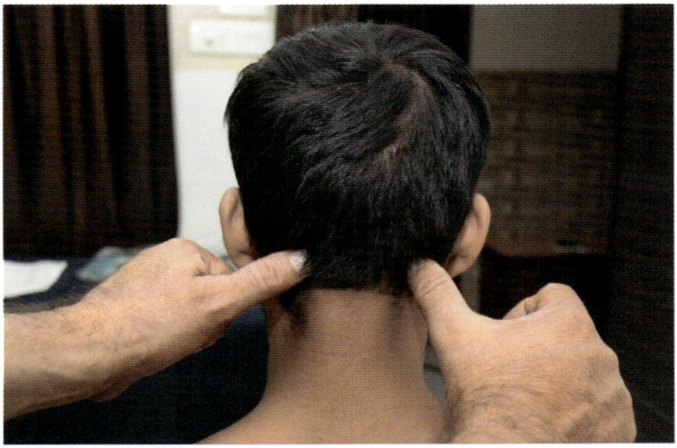

The position of Krikatika marma is on the back of head at the junction of neck and head. These are two in number.

**RESPONSIBLE SIRA BINDU:** Sira of pittashay dhamani (GB20)

**Another possibility:** Du15, Du16

**INDICATIONS:** According to Sushrut Sharir 6/27

*Tatra chalmurdhata.*

तत्र चलमूर्धता

सुश्रुत शारीर 6/27

This marma has its indications for dizziness, vertigo, mental disorders etc.

## KRIKATIKA MARMA CHIKITSA

For above said indications, following methods can be used:

1. **VIMLAPAN:** Press marmas of both sides simultaneously with the help of thumb of both hands.
2. **AGNIKARM:** Mild heat stimulation with the help of *dhoop* stick or moxa.

# Marma and their responsible Sira Bindu

| S. No. | Name of Marma | Sira Bindu (Meridian Points) Comparative Chinese Acupuncture points | |
|---|---|---|---|
| 1. | Talhridaya Marma | H8, P8 | Upper Extremity |
| | | K1 | Lower Extremity |
| 2. | Indravasti Marma | P4 | Upper Extremity |
| | | UB58, GB35 | Lower Extremity |
| 3. | Gud Marma | Du1, Ren1 | |
| 4. | Stanrohit Marma | St16, Sp20 | |
| 5. | Neela | St9 | |
| 6 | Manya | LI18 | |
| 7. | Matrika | | |
| 8. | Shringatak Marma | UB4, St8, GB4 | |
| | | UB5, GB15, Du22,23 | |
| 9. | Apang Marma | GB1, Sj23 | |
| 10. | Sthapani Marma | Not in regular channel | |
| 11. | Phana Marma | LI19, LI20 | |
| 12. | Stanmool Marma | St18, Sp17, K22 | |
| 13. | Apalap Marma | Lu1 | |
| 14. | Apastambha Marma | Sp19 | |

| S. No | Name of Marma | Sira Bindu (Meridian Points) Comparative Chinese Acupuncture points | |
|---|---|---|---|
| 15. | Hridaya Marma | Ren14, Ren15 | |
| 16. | Nabhi Marma | Ren7, Ren8, Ren9 Backshu UB15 | |
| 17. | Parshvasandhi Marma | GB26 | |
| 18. | Brihati Marma | UB18 | |
| 19. | Lohitaksha Marma | H1 | Upper Extremity |
| | | Liv11 | Lower Extremity |
| 20. | Urvi Marma | P2 | Upper Extremity |
| | | UB37 | Lower Extremity |
| 21. | Ani Marma | LI12, Sj11 | Upper Extremity |
| | | GB31, St33 | Lower Extremity |
| 22. | Vitap Marma | K11, Ren2 | |
| 23. | Kakshdhar Marma | Extraordinary point | |
| 24. | Kurch Marma | SI2, SI3, Sj2, Sj3, LI3 | Upper Extremity |
| | | GB41,GB42,GB43,St43 | Lower Extremity |
| 25. | Kurchshir Marma | Sj4, SI4 | Upper Extremity |
| | | GB40, St41 | Lower Extremity |
| 26. | Vasti Marma | Ren3, Ren4, Ren5, Ren6 | |
| 27. | Kshipra Marma | LI4 | Upper Extremity |
| | | Liv2, Liv3 | Lower Extremity |
| 28. | Ans Marma | GB21 | |
| 29. | Utkshep Marma | Near St8 (Not in regular channel) | |
| 30. | Vidhur Marma | Sj16, Sj17 | |

| S. No | Name of Marma | Sira Bindu (Meridian Points) Comparative Chinese Acupuncture points |
|---|---|---|
| 31. | Katiktarun Marma | UB31, UB32, UB53 |
| 32. | Nitamb Marma | GB30 |
| 33. | Ansphalak Marma | UB11, UB41 |
| 34. | Shankh Marma | Not in regular channel |
| 35. | Janu Marma | GB32, GB34, UB40, St34, St35 Lat. Aspect<br>K10, Liv7, Liv8, Sp9, Sp10 Med. Aspect |
| 36. | Kurpar Marma | LI11, Sj10, SI8 |
| 37. | Simant Marma | Not in regular Channel<br>Extraordinary point(Sishencong) |
| 38. | Adhipati Marma | Du20 |
| 39. | Gulph Marma | GB39, UB59 Lateral Aspect<br>K3, Sp5 Medial Aspect |
| 40. | Manibandh Marma | SI5, Sj5, LI5 Dorsal Aspect<br>Lu9, P7 Ventral Aspect |
| 41. | Kukundar Marma | GB29 |
| 42. | Avart Marma | GB14 |
| 43. | Krikatika Marma | GB20 (other possibility Du15, D16) |

# Glossary

| | | |
|---|---|---|
| Adhah | : | Downward, below |
| Adhimanth | : | Severe pain and irritation of eyes, causing severe headache in half of the head with other characteristic signs |
| Agneya | : | Hot and dry in nature |
| Agnikarma | : | Heat treatment (moxibustion) |
| Akshi | : | Eye |
| Alpa shukrata | : | Oligospermia |
| Andhya | : | Blindness |
| Angasad | : | Exhaustion of a body part or body |
| Angul | : | Finger (unit of measurement) |
| Anguli | : | Finger |
| Angushth | : | Toe |
| Arasagrahita | : | Tastelessness |
| Ardh | : | Half |
| Artav nadi | : | Female dominating channel (Ren Channel of Chinese) |
| Ashmari | : | Calculus |
| Asthi | : | Bone |
| Asthi shosh | : | Osteoporosis |

| | | |
|---|---|---|
| Avedhya | : | Should not be pierced |
| Badhiryam | : | Deafness |
| Bhru | : | Eyebrow |
| Bhrupucchant | : | Lateral end of eyebrow |
| Drishti | : | Sight |
| Gandh | : | Smell |
| Ghran | : | Nose |
| Greeva | : | Neck |
| Gud | : | Anal area |
| Gulph desh | : | Area of ankle joint |
| Hast | : | Hand |
| Heen roop | : | Deficient in form or beauty, defective appearance |
| Jangha | : | Shank |
| Jihva | : | Tongue |
| Kalantar pranhar | : | Fatal after some time |
| Kanth nadi | : | Trachea |
| Karn | : | Ear |
| Karn shool | : | Earache |
| Kasa shvasa | : | Cough and breathing trouble |
| Kati | : | Loin |
| Khanj | : | Lameness |
| Koshth | : | Torso, hollow organ |
| Kshar | : | Alkali |
| Kunthata | : | Maimed (handicapped related to hand) |
| Lalat | : | Forehead |
| Lohitpoornata | : | Filled with blood |

| | | |
|---|---|---|
| Madhye | : | In between |
| Manibandh | : | Area of wrist joint |
| Mans | : | Flesh, muscles |
| Maranam | : | Death |
| Medhra | : | Penis |
| Mook | : | Dumb |
| Mriyate | : | To death |
| Mutra | : | Urine |
| Mutrashay | : | Urinary bladder |
| Nirsan | : | To excrete |
| Pad | : | Foot |
| Pakshaghat | : | Paralysis of one side |
| Pakvashay | : | The seat of digested food |
| Pandu | : | Dusty pale, anaemic, yellowish white, jaundiced |
| Pani | : | Hand |
| Parshni | : | Heel |
| Parshva | : | Sides, flank, the outer sides of ribs |
| Payu | : | Anal orifice |
| Pratibaddh | : | Joints |
| Prishtha | : | Back |
| Prishtha vansh | : | Vertebral column (backbone) |
| Ruja | : | Pain |
| Rujakar | : | Related to pain |
| Sadhya Pranhar | : | Instant death |
| Sakthi | : | Lower extremity |
| Sakthi shosh | : | Atrophy of muscles and tissues of extremity |

| | | |
|---|---|---|
| Sandhi | : | Junction, joint |
| Sandhan | : | To join |
| Shakha | : | Extremities |
| Shandhya | : | Impotency |
| Shankh Pradesh | : | Temporal area of head |
| Shat | : | Hundreds of |
| Shonit | : | Blood |
| Shoph | : | Swelling |
| Shroni | : | The hip, Loins |
| Shukra Nadi | : | Male dominating Channel |
| Sira | : | Ends, Heads, A stream |
| Siravyadhan | : | Therapeutic puncture (Acupuncture) |
| Snayu | : | Ligament, tendon, muscle, nerve, vein |
| Snehadi | : | Oil etc. |
| Snehan | : | Oleation, Specific pre panchkarma procedure |
| Stabdh bahuta | : | Numbness of upper extremity |
| Stabdh sakthita | : | Numbness of lower extremity |
| Stan | : | Breast |
| Stan choochuk | : | Nipple |
| Sushrut | : | Amongst one of the learned disciple of Dhanvantari |
| Swapanital Kunchit | | |
| Sammit | : | The area formed while contracting the palm (6.0 to 7.0 cm) |
| Svarvaikrit | : | Hoarseness of voice |
| Svedan | : | This is a specific prepanchkarma |

| | | |
|---|---|---|
| | | procedure in which heat or medicated steam is used |
| Trik | : | Joints of three bones sacroiliac as well as cervicoscapular joint |
| Trishna | : | Thirst |
| Ubhayatah | : | Both sides |
| Udar | : | Abdomen |
| Upasth | : | External genitalia |
| Upghata | : | Damage, violation |
| Urdhva jatru | : | Above clavicle |
| Uru | : | Thigh |
| Va | : | or |
| Vaikalya | : | Imperfection, defectiveness |
| Vaksh | : | Chest, torso |
| Varch | : | Faecal matter (stool) |
| Vedhan | : | Puncturing, piercing |
| Varna | : | Colour |
| Vran | : | A wound, sore, ulcer, abcess, tumour, boil, scar |
| Vrishan | : | Scrotum |

# Bibliography


1. Ashtang Sangrah, Dr. Ravidatt Tripathi, Chowkhamba Sanskrit Pratishthan, Delhi
2. Atridev (Ed) Sushrut Samhita, Motilal Banarasidas Delhi 1975
3. B. D. Chaurasia's Human Anatomy, C.B.S. Publishers & Distributors Pvt Ltd, New Delhi
4. Charak Samhita, Pt. Kashinath Pandeya, Dr. Gorakhnath Chaturvedi, Chowkhamba Vidya Bhavan, Varanasi-1
5. Dr Ambica dutt Shastri (Ed) Sushrut Samhita, Chowkhamba Sanskrit Sansthan, Varanasi 985
6. Essentials of Chinese Acupuncture, Foreign language press, Beijing
7. Harrison's Principles of Internal Medicine, McGraw Hill Education
8. Parishadyam Shabdarth Shariram
9. M. Monier-Williams, Sanskrit English Dictionary Motilal Banarasidas, Delhi 1999
10. Rigveda Part 4, Acharya Vedanta Teerth, Manoj Publications, Fifth edition 2015
11. Vaman Shivram Apte, Sanskrit Hindi Kosh, Oriental Book Centre, Delhi 1997
12. Vedic Health Care System Dr.Ram Lal Sah, Dr Binod Kumar Joshi, Dr Geeta Joshi, New Age Books, New Delhi, 2002

# Index